MY NAME IS
Tina

Maria Abi Hamad Khoury

Fulton Books, Inc.
Meadville, PA

Published by Fulton Books 2021

ISBN 978-1-63985-047-1 (paperback)
ISBN 978-1-63985-048-8 (digital)

Printed in the United States of America

Synopsis

This is the story of a young girl who lost her voice and identity and eventually found them. It is a story of struggle, abuse, and redemption. Tina grew up in a middle-class American family. She resented her family and her life. She embroiled her parents in many bad situations. She called the cops on them, and they nearly lost custody of their children. She attended nursing school and became active in the political scene. She became abusive toward all those who opposed her political views. While in college she met and fell in love with a refugee from Iraq. She converted to his religion, changed her name to Aisha, and married him and dropped out of college in her senior year. She became a strong advocate of radical Islam.

She alienated herself from her friends and family. She refused to have anything to do with her family, going as far as calling the police on them. In her eyes they were infidels trying to sway her from the path of enlightenment. She gave birth to a little girl, Amira, and went on a visit with his husband and his family back to Iraq (Mosul). During her visit, Mosul came under the rule of ISIS. At first, she was ecstatic and did all she could to show her support of ISIS. In Mosul, the blinds were ripped from her eyes. Her husband became extremely abusive toward her. Secrets and lies were revealed about her husband and his family. She discovered that her husband's sister was his wife, and his nephew and nieces were his children. She also endured the horrors of ISIS rule. She regretted all her previous actions. She longed for her family and country. Realizing the error of her actions, she prayed for deliverance from the nightmare she found herself in. Finally, with the help of her husband, she escaped back to the USA with her daughter and two stepdaughters.

Back in the USA, she had another fight on her hands. Her siblings did not want anything to do with her. She tried to connect with them, but they could not bring themselves to forgive her for what she put her family through. Her parents supported her and the children. They insisted she finish her nursing degree and attend therapy. She was once again on her own. Her siblings and their families rejected her. She knew that it would take much work to bridge the gap between them. Her siblings relented, and she was accepted back into the fold of her family. Ultimately, she found love with a colleague of hers, got married, and moved in with him.

Contents

Prologue

My journey started when we were no more than young adults, thinking we could take the world and everything it threw at us. Little did we know we were ill-equipped to deal with the reality of life outside our little safe cocoon. We strutted around, boasting to everyone who listened of our plans to conquer the world. In our minds, no one could stand in our way. We were full of bravado and in my opinion idiocy. We knew everything there was to know and had an opinion on everything and everyone. We were the elite and wanted to change the world to our way of thinking. We were going to prove the naysayers wrong. We could do whatever we wanted, and no one could stop us. We grew up in a society that told us we can do no wrong, and there was little or no consequences to our actions. We thought that by taking a couple of classes at university about different religions and cultures, we became experts on the subjects at hand. We could travel anywhere in the world and become part of the culture without any problems. We could gain any person's respect and acceptance of us because we are deeply knowledgeable and smart.

Some good-intentioned people tried to warn us about our naive view of the world, but to no avail. In our opinion, these people were bigots trying to hinder humans from going forward. We needed to break the binds of slavery that were keeping us in the Dark Ages. These people wanted to scare us to keep us in check. What did these people know? They were ignorant and set in their ways. They were not aware of the fact that the world had changed so drastically, and that these cultures we were going to visit and live in, were open, and more accepting than our own American culture. These cultures

1

respect and revere women and children. We can prove it, because we have met individuals from these cultures, and they were nice to us. These individuals—and we rank them among our closest friends— have explained to us all about their culture and how it is much more superior to our decadent Western culture. We took their word as gospel and did not question their own version of the truth. This is my story.

Looking around, all I saw was the injustices perpetuated by our corrupt, capitalist, racist system. Some people had it all, while others struggled to put food on the table. This system needed to be torn down and replaced by a more equitable system that distributed wealth among all echelons of society.

Tina was my name.

Tina was my name, but I have not heard anyone call me by that name in an exceptionally long time. Every night when I manage to go to sleep, I dream of my family and friends back in the US. I pray every day for a way out of this living hell I am in but see no ray of hope. My life as I knew it a year ago seized to exit. I am a prisoner in this desolate land. I gave up any rights I had when I married a local Muslim man. I am nothing but a chattel to his whims. I am wife number three and in a couple of weeks, he will take wife number four. I thought I was special and valued above all else, but little did I know I was nothing but a warm body and an available womb for his seed to fertilize and produce fruit. He sees me as an object for his desires and sexual release. My husband beats and starves me for the slightest perceived infringement on my part. I am living a horror story every second of my long day. Sleeping has become a luxury I could ill afford these days. I never know what the household of terror is up to when I am not awake. I am living in fear of losing my daughter and being cast out on the streets for other fighters to tear into me like salivating animals. My husband has constantly threatened to divorce me, rip my child from my bosom, and sell me as a sexual slave to his men. I am terrified of losing my daughter and forced to service his men.

With great fear and frustration, I asked my husband Jalal: "Why would you give me to your men, is it not against your religion to do that?"

Looking at me with lust and a voice full of contempt and disrespect, he replied, "It is not up to you to decide what to do, you Christian whore, it is the will of Allah that a husband knows best what to do. A good and obedient wife does the will of her husband. Never ever question me again, you infidel whore. You should be honored that I married you. You are nothing but the refuse that should be cast aside. You were nothing before I married you. I showed you the path of truth as given to us by our holy prophet God, praise him. The greatest honor can bestow on anyone is to convert him to the true religion of Islam. What I have given you is the most precious thing on this earth. Do not you see when you disobey me, you are disobeying God and his prophet. It is forbidden in Islam for a wife to question her husband."

Once upon a time in defiance I asked him, "Why would a man beat his wife, if according to your beliefs women were respected and protected in Islam?"

He punched him in the belly and replied, "Do not question me again. According Shiekh Saad Arafat, Allah honored wives by instating the punishment of beatings." The Prophet Mohammad said, "Do not beat her in the face, and do not make her ugly. Islam forbids it. Show her she is honored. If the husband beats his wife, he must not beat her in the face. Even when he beats her, he must not curse her. This is incredible! He beats her to discipline her. In addition, there must not be more than ten beatings, and he must not break her bones, injure her, break her teeth, or poke her in the eye. There is quite an etiquette to the beatings. If he beats her to discipline her, he must not raise his hand high. He must beat her from the chest level. All this honor the women. She is need of discipline. How should the husband discipline her? Through admonishment. If she is not deterred, he should refuse to share the bed with her. If she is not repentant, he should beat her, but there are rules to the beating. If he beats her, the beatings should not be hard, so that they do not leave a mark. He can beat her with a short rod."

3

I feared a brutal beating after the speech Jalal gave me on wife beating. I knew he was not gentle in his beatings no matter what he said. I did not trust him not to show any compassion. His beatings were becoming more and more vicious every day. I did not believe any word he uttered. I was convinced he was a brutal individual who was able to prove his strength by intimidating individuals weaker than him.

I cast my eyes down to the floor and, with a beseeching voice, asked Jalil, "But to give me to service your men, is that not considered prostitution in the holy Quran?"

Jalal grew terribly angry with me, and for that I was brutally beaten and raped right on the floor of our sitting area, without a thought to who might witness this horrific act.

"I beseech you, Jalal, stop. Please stop, I cannot take it anymore," I cried. "Show mercy to your humble wife. Whatever you want I will do. Please I beg you stop."

He kept at it until I was bruised and bleeding all over. I kept begging for mercy, asking him to stop his brutal assault, but my pleas fell on deaf ears. He did not care how much he was hurting me. All he cared about was attaining his own pleasure.

After he finished his heinous deed, he kicked me in my rips and spat on me, telling me to never question his edicts, saying in a condescending voice, "What does an American whore know of the truth? You are nothing but a product of the corrupt infidel Christian world, with all its idols, sluts, and decaying morals."

He further threatened me, saying, "When I cast you aside like a bone to the dogs, I shall take your daughter from you, and marry her off to my leader. He will appreciate a blue-eyed, blond-haired bride. He can bring her up as he sees fit, docile and obedient, unlike her whore of a mother. When she starts her menses, then he can be a true husband to her.

"Remember well that I married you to sleep with you. I lusted after you because you dressed and behaved like a common slut. All I wanted was your body. Your forward manner disgusted me, but I wanted you sexually and still do. If it were not for the fact that I still find you sexually desirable, I would have cast you aside a long time ago."

I was in such pain that I could do nothing but beg him to stop his vicious tirade. His attack on me was unprovoked. How can I live like this? A vessel for this unscrupulous man to slake his sexual needs on. A punching bag for his frustrations and disappointments.

Finally, bruised and blooded, I lost consciousness and fell to the floor, with my six-month-old daughter beside me screaming and crying for me. I woke up barely able to move from the severe beating inflicted on my person. I tried holding my daughter to my chest, but I could not summon the strength to do so. I was afraid her screaming and crying might bring on another about of physical abuse. From my position on the floor, I could see my husband's other two wives hurling abuse at my person. One of them, Um Hammoudi, number one wife, went so far as to spit in my face.

Um Hammoudi: "What did you expect, you American Christian whore? You are nothing here. Do you understand? Nothing. We pray to Allah every day for him to cast you aside. We curse the day he met you. You do not know our ways and traditions. Did you think you are anything special? I hope you die."

I knew Um Hammoudi was upset because she was his favorite bride before I came along. Even though Jalal did not love or respect me, he desired me sexually. He did spend more time with me than both his other wives. Both wives resented this fact. They were afraid he would get rid of one of them and keep me. They tried their best to create problems where none existed. They fabricated lies about me. They rushed to Jalal whenever the opportunity arose to tell him these untruths. They thought that by sleeping with me, Jalal was showing me great honor. Believe me, I could do without such an honor.

I shrugged off their insults. I kept thinking if they only knew how much I resented them and their way of life. Little did they know that I would gladly walk away from Jalal if given the chance. I hated him with a vengeance. All I wanted was to take myself and daughter away from this life of degradation. If they thought I wanted Jalal, then they were way off the mark. Jalil disgusted me; they disgusted me.

Their upbringing is such that they thought their husband's word is law. His wants, desires, and needs needed to be catered to. A woman's role was to do what her husband wants.

It was with utter disgust and incredulity the first time I realized I was one of three wives Jalil had. I was shocked at how gullible I was. It is a story I would leave for another time and place.

Both wives turned their backs on me and my little daughter and went about their duties. I gathered my baby to me and crawled to the corner of the room with tears streaming down my face. I was in such agony that I could barely keep conscious.

Strong for My Daughter

I knew I needed to stay strong and vigilant for my daughter's sake. I was terrified that her father will rip her from my arms and sell her to the highest bidder. I needed to plan and bide my time and plan my escape from this living hell. I also knew that my fair complexion, blond hair, and blue eyes were my biggest asset. Even though my husband abused me, he was still sexually attracted to me. He would not cast me aside easily.

I would use his sexual attraction to me to keep myself and my daughter safe for the time being. I felt repelled by his touch, but I had no other choice but to submit to his demands. He was hoping to impregnate me with his son. Every time I thought of this, I felt sick to my stomach. I could not think of a worse fate than to bare him a son in his image. It nearly killed me to give birth to his daughter, who thankfully resembled me greatly. But a son bearing my husband's name and looks, I could not fathom even the thought.

Finally, I slept with my daughter clutched to my bosom. During the night, Jalal dragged me from a fretful sleep and in front of my daughter forced himself on me. He shoved me aside like a used rag after he finished his heinous deed. He just walked away and entered Um Hammoudi's bedroom to spend the rest of the night with her.

I felt violated and cheap. He just treated me like a cheap whore. I crawled to the bathroom and threw up. I tried to cleanse myself from his touch. I have become what he made me—a slave to his whims. I was disgusted with myself and him.

Crawling back to the corner of the living room, where my daughter and I slept, I collapsed on my mattress next to my daughter.

He might rape and abuse me daily, but I knew that I could use his actions to my advantage. Eventually he would let down his guard, and I would be able to get away. The hatred brewing in my heart could be justified by Jalal's treatment of me. I kept thinking of the sorry state my life has come to. Oh! Why did I think I knew it all? I was so stupid and naive. I scoffed at the people who told me the truth. I belittled my culture and country. I was such a stupid idiot who thought the world revolved around her. I shall regret my stupidity for the rest of my life.

Abou Shibil

I was jarred from a restless sleep by sounds coming from outside. A young man was crying and begging for mercy. His cries were echoing all around. I edged toward the window with my daughter clutched to my bosom, to see what all the commotion was all about. What met my eyes was a scene from the Middle Ages. A mob of bearded men were dragging a young man to the center of the village square. The young man looked terrified to death of these bearded man. While they were dragging him through the streets, they were kicking and punching him all over his body. He was blooded and bruised all over. I began shaking with fear and was revolted at these men's actions. They were abusing this poor young man while at the same time screaming al Takbir: "Allah Akbar," "God is great."

When they reached the center square one of the bearded men stood aside to declare the sins that this young man was accused of. I recognized the bearded man as Abu Shibil, the leader of the fighters in the area. He was a hard-line fanatic, who hated anyone who did not adhere to his vision of the world. He frightened me to death.

Abu Shibil was the man that Jalal threatened to give my daughter to. Abu Shibil had complete control over his men. He had brainwashed them to his way of thinking. His word was law. If anyone dared to question his dictates, they were declared heretics and met a slow and painful death.

Having lived among these people for more than two years, I had become fluent in their language. As I listened to the man's sins being read out, I was shocked to my very essence. It seems this poor man had refused the request of the self-appointed Khalif, or leader of these extremists, to marry his underage daughter.

9

This man had committed the ultimate sin. The girl in question was only nine years of age. According to Abu Shibil, he was the successor of the prophet, and thus had the divine right to marry whom he wants. Citing from the Hadith, he reminded everyone that the prophet married Aisha, the Khalif Omar's daughter, when she was six years of age, and slept with her when she started her menses, at the age of nine. The prophet, peace be upon him, was fifty-four years old. According to Sahih Bukhari Volume 7, Book 62, Number 88:

> Narrated 'Ursa: The Prophet wrote the (marriage contract) with 'Aisha while she was six years old and consummated his marriage with her while she was nine years old and she remained with him for nine years (i.e., till his death).

Abu Shibil said that he had a dream that this girl was destined to be his wife. In the Hadith Sahih Bukhar 9.140:

> Narrated 'Aisha: Allah's Apostle said to me, "You were shown to me twice (in my dream) before I married you. I saw an angel carrying you in a silken piece of cloth, and I said to him, 'Uncover (her),' and behold, it was you. I said (to myself), 'If this is from Allah, then it must happen."

Abu Shibil: "In the name of Alllah and as the Khalif of this Islamic State, I Abu Shibil, decree that this man has disobeyed the edicts of our religion. In his ignorance and selfness, he has deemed himself above our laws and as a result has committed a heinous crime. He dared to question rules that were given to us by God Almighty through our Prophet Mohammad, Salam aliehi Allah wa salam [praised by God]. We as followers of the prophet will not tolerate anyone going against our dictates."

He paused for a minute and then in a high, shrill voice said, "I order this man to be stripped bare and given one hundred lashes for his ignorance and disrespect of the successor of the Prophet God, praise him. This should be a lesson to those who dare question my dictates and wisdom. If the prophet, in his wisdom, deemed it permissible, then all his successors need to follow in his footsteps."

Abu Shibil took a deep breath and continued his speech: "Within an hour, his daughter will be escorted to my house and given to me as bride. It is an honor I bestow on you. I could have chosen any women, but God in his wisdom has chosen your daughter Samira for my wife. Let it be a lesson to all who oppose God's wisdom. Allah Akbar, I have spoken."

The man was stripped to the waist, held, and his hands tied to a post in the center of the square. Abu Shibil gave the signal, and his man began administering the punishment. I could not watch anymore. I felt nauseous and faint. I collapsed on the floor next to the window, with the man's screams of agony echoing in my ears. The poor man, in trying to protect his daughter from rape from a brutal and inhumane man, was sanctioned to receive a severe thrashing. What an unfair and unjust man. I could not stand it anymore.

It was not the first time I had witnessed such vicious and inhumane behavior from Abou Shibel and his men. The mere mention of his name sent shivers down my spine. Jalal was the only person standing between me and this monster. I always knew that he lusted after me. He had seen me with Jalal before I had converted to Islam. He knew what I looked like, and he wanted to possess me. Jalal was one of his men, and I knew it was a matter of time before Jalal broke under the pressure Abou Shibel put on him. Jalal would divorce me and hand me over to Abou Shibel to become his sexual plaything. I also knew that Jalal, to gain favor with Abou Shibel, had promised my baby daughter to him. He will hand her over to Abou Shibel when she started her menstrual cycle.

I had seen other young girls being bartered for favors. Affluent older men seek young, malleable girls as brides. These men were sexual predators, using religion to cater to their own sexual perversions. They wanted young virgin brides to initiate and impregnate with their children to prove their manhood to the world. These young innocents had little choice on the matter. These poor girls were a little better than slaves to be sold to the highest bidder. More times than not these girls ended up being pregnant and cast aside by their older husbands in favor of younger girls. These girls were then passed along to other men. What a life these girls had to face. I felt for them, and it hurt just thinking that my life and the life of my daughter would follow the same path.

It was a nightmare living with this constant fear. My future was not safe. I did not know from one day to the next what was going to happen to me and my daughter. My fate was in the hands of a religiously crazed, brainwashed individual. My situation was not unique. Most females living under the rule of these monsters shared a similar fate. They were forced to adhere to a version of Islam that came from the Middle Ages. Even their parents could not protect them from the wrath of these inhuman, uncivilized monsters. It was frightening and degrading to realize what lengths these monsters would go to implement their perverted view of their interpretation of Islam.

Tears streamed down my eyes, my heartbeat increased drastically, and my hands started sweating. What can anyone do in the face of such injustice? How can we stand up to these barbarians? The image of my poor and helpless daughter meeting the same fate as this poor girl kept coming to my mind. I needed to get away from here, back to my family, friends, and to my beloved country that I had abandoned with such gusto.

I now realize what I have left behind. A country that gave me freedom to choose how to live my life. A country that respected my choices no matter what they were. I never realized how great my country was until I turned my back on it. I made a vow to myself to go down on my knees and kiss the ground of my beloved country when I escaped from this hell. I cut ties with a family that loved and cared for me. A father and mother who sacrificed a lot to give us the best in life. A Christian religion that taught about love and acceptance of others. A culture that respected me as an individual and as a woman. I gave up my studies and future for this living hell. What have I done to myself? I realized that I was my worst enemy.

In secret, I prayed the Lord's Prayer and Hail Mary, asking God to help me through this difficult time in my life. I asked God to help through this difficult time in my life and promised him I would never abandon my beliefs again.

Tina

I grew up in a middle-class Irish Catholic family. My parents were loving and supportive of their children. We were two boys and a girl. I was the baby of the family. I was eight years younger than Sam, my older brother, and six years younger than David, my younger brother. I was the princess in my family. Both my parents and brothers treated me like spun glass. I was the beloved daughter and younger sister in the family. I could do no wrong. My every whim was indulged. I was protected and cosseted. My brothers adored me. I grew up thinking the world owed me something.

My parents both held down jobs. My mother was an elementary teacher, and my father was a contractor. They worked hard to support us and instill in us a good moral upbringing. I guess we were like any other middle-class family in the US. We only attended church twice a year, at Christmas and Easter. We were what is commonly known as CE (Christmas and Easter) Catholics. I still had a great childhood. On Sundays we went to my grandparents' house and had lunch with the whole extended family. I loved Sundays because I got to play with all my cousins.

In high school I got exposed to different values than the ones I had grown up with. Drugs, gangs, and sex were ramped. The atmosphere was such that being moral was looked down at. Our sex education teachers told us that it was not wrong to have intercourse if you protect yourself. The message that came was abstaining from sex was not normal. Students' who did not know any better and were ill-equipped to deal with the emotional aspect of any sexual relationship were often at a loss at what to do when their relationships went sour.

Girls were the ones that often paid the heavy price of these relationships. If any of them got pregnant, the boy usually went on with his life as if nothing really happened. On the other hand, the girl had to change her whole life to accommodate this new development.

In retrospect, I could see that these teenage kids did not live their life to the fullest. They grew up much too fast. They did not experience the innocence of their teenage years. There was no one to disciple us growing up. It was the norm for us to mock our teachers. Laws had been put into place to hinder the ability of teachers to discipline their students. All these laws were put into place in the name of progress and knowing what is best for the students. No taboo was preserved, and all behaviors were accepted. Students needed to express themselves, and that was more important than discipline. Excuses were always found for bad behavior.

I remember one incident clearly that left an impression on me. I was in class one day, and the teacher asked us to please be quiet so that he could explain a complicated math problem. This was an honor class, and we all needed to get good grades. One student refused to listen to the teacher. When the teacher asked him again to be quiet, the student stood up and said, "Fuck you."

Stunned, the teacher asked the student to leave the classroom.

The student got out of his chair, stared at the teacher with contempt, walked out of the classroom, and banged the door after him. We all were stunned by such behavior. We all thought the student would be expelled for sure. I felt that the student's parents would surely punish this young man.

To our great astonishment, a few days later the same student was back in class. Instead of being punished, the teacher was reprimanded by the school administration because he impinged on the student's right to speech right. It seems that, in the name of free speech, any student or individual can express themselves as vocally as they wanted. On the other hand, the teacher needed to be overly cautious of what he or she says because it might hurt and upset the students. Teachers needed to be incredibly careful in voicing their opinion because it might influence students' minds.

Calling the Police on My Parents

This was the environment I grew up in. I felt that I was entitled to my rights. I never for one second thought I needed to earn these rights. This feeling of entitlement prevailed with most of my generation for the longest time.

I wanted to go out partying with my friends. My parents did not agree with me. When I started screaming and shouting at them. They did not give in, like they usually did, and were adamant that I would not be allowed to leave the house. In my typically vindictive manner, I accused my parents of child abuse. I threatened to call the police. My parents who thought I could do no wrong did not believe that their beautiful child would do such a thing. They thought that I was throwing a tantrum, but I went through with my threat and called the police on them.

I called the police and told them that I was afraid of my parents, and that they were being abusive toward me.

Tina: "Please come and help me, my parents are being very abusive, and I fear for my life."

911 operative: "Please calm down, are you in immediate danger at the moment?"

Tina crying: "Yes, please come."

911 operative: "We are on our way, please try to stay calm and out of harm's way."

I was incredibly pleased with myself for standing up for my rights. No one had the right to tell me what to do. My head was full of grandiose ideas about my place in the world. If I wanted to use profanities, go out partying, hook up with my boyfriends, or stay out late, no one had the right to tell me no. I wanted to teach my parents a lesson they could not forget. I wanted to scare them so badly that they never raised their voices to me or told me what to do. I knew it all, and they were just a pair of old-fashioned idiots who do not know what they are doing. These sentiments were brewing very strongly in me. I wanted to be the queen of the world, and no one had any right to stand in my way.

Within fifteen minutes the police had arrived at our doorstep. They banged at the door and demanded to see me and my parents.

The police officer looked at my father suspiciously. "We just got a hysterical call from you daughter, Tina, claiming that she is in fear for her life."

Jim was taken aback by the officer accusation and in a shocked voice said, "Excuse me officer, but I think you have the wrong house."

Shaking his head at my father, the officer replied, "I am sorry, sir, we need to talk to your daughter Tina to make sure she is not in any danger."

Getting a bit defensive, my father could not accept what he was hearing. There must be something wrong. His beautiful daughter was home safe. No one has harmed her. He thought someone must be playing a prank on him. An unbelievably bad one at that. "Officer, I assure you my daughter is perfectly fine."

Ignoring my father's words, the officer insisted on talking to me. "Sir, we need to see you daughter and take you to the police station to investigate this situation. Child Services will be here shortly."

Aghast and not comprehending the situation, in an agitated voice, my father started questioning the police officer. "What are you talking about? Why are Child Services coming here? What is going on here? I assure my daughter Tina is perfectly safe, and no one had threatened or harmed her. Why are you doing this?"

In an authoritative voice that brooked no argument, the officer said, "We need to remove your children from your care and investigate child abuse claims made by your daughter against you and your wife."

My dad looked at my poor mother for help, but she was just as shocked as he was. They both thought this was a bad dream.

They could not comprehend the situation. Their own daughter had reported them to the police for child abuse.

Little did I know what was in store for my family. My parents were dragged to the police station to answer to the false charges I had made. My brothers and I were taken into the child-service custody and then released to my grandparents' care. I was terrified of all these events. I did not know that my act of rebellion would result in so much chaos. My parents had to endure months of interrogation before they could prove they were fit parents.

I was too scared to admit my lies and had to stand by as all these events unraveled before my eyes. My brothers were upset and blamed me for all this. They both knew that I was in the wrong and refused to talk to me. My parents tried their best to bridge the gap I had created in our family fabric, but to no avail. I was still unrepentant. I thought that I had achieved a great feat. Instead of being severely punished for my lies, I was being treated as if I were made of spun glass.

I lost respect for any authority figure in my life, because deep down I knew I had the upper hand in all dealings. My parents were too frightened of losing their children to discipline me. It empowered me to think that I was above the law and that my actions would have little consequences.

College (I Knew It All)

When I finished high school, I was accepted at a prestigious college in the Northeast. In college I found my own niche. I was on cloud nine with my new friends and newfound ideas and ideals. I was exposed to new ideas, and became passionate about many different causes. I became an activist. I would demonstrate against any injustice I deemed was worth my while. I became a crusader for all causes I deemed worthy of my attention. I wanted to make my mark on the world. I saw myself as another Gandhi, liberating the world of all oppressive forces.

I started a campaign against all religious symbols in our school. I circulated a petition against a college professor who wore a cross around her neck. I was adamant that that professor had no right to demonstrate any kind of religious affiliation during her time in the lecture hall. In my opinion, she was imposing her views on others. She had no right to shove her religion down our throats. I wanted to show the world how open-minded I was. I was a free spirit. I wanted no restraints on my growth as an individual.

We harassed the poor professor until she resigned her position as a lecturer in college. Little did I know the harm I had inflicted on this poor person. Karma was a thing to fear. My action had consequences that I had not foreseen. This episode was going to haunt me for a long time. The great warrior I perceived myself to be was nothing but a bully hiding behind self-righteousness and false moral superiority. If only I can go back in time and give my stupid, selfish, and young self a smack.

I felt I had won a great war against these backward religious Christians that wanted to brainwash us and keep us in the Dark Ages. Christianity in my opinion was the worst doctrine to spread in our society. The Church, especially then Catholic Church, degraded women, opposed gays rights, and opposed progress. This corrupt ideology has in the past destroyed great civilizations. Like any other person arguing the Church, I brought up the Spanish Inquisition and how it tortured and hurt all people who opposed the Church, especially the Jews.

One student challenged me to target a professor who wore the veil. She asked me, "Why did you target the professor wearing the cross? There is another professor who wears the veil, and the veil is a religious symbol."

I looked at her as if she lost her mind.

"Do not be such a racist. You are an Islamophobic. Do you not realize that Christianity is the bane of civilization? From its inception it has taken over the world, murdered people, oppressed women, degraded people of power, and destroyed all that came before it." I continued with my pontification on the evils of Christianity and the tolerance of other religions such as Islam and Judaism. "When the Prophet Mohammad came, he spread peace and tolerance to all nations."

When the same student tried arguing with me, I shut her down with my loud and obnoxious personality.

"If that is the case," the student trying to reason with me said, "why are women treated like second citizens? They are forced to wear the hijab, stoned to death for adultery, forced into arranged marriages, raped and killed daily."

I looked at him in scorn and said, "That is just ridiculous. Where do you get this information? I cannot believe your idiotic ideas."

"Well, what about torturing and killing gay people in the Islamic world? Is that not well-documented fact, or are you so blind to your prejudices that you refuse to accept these facts?"

I could not answer his comeback, but being the social warrior, I went on counterattack: "Look what the Catholic Church did to the world. The Church started wars, oppressed people, forcibly converted whole populations, and launched the Crusades against innocent people, all in the name of the Christian faith. You are nothing but a hater, an ignorant idiot who has not read and analyzed historical events."

When the same student tried to point out the errors of my argument, citing well-known documents, I walked away from her, screaming profanities and insults.

"Oh my God!" I screamed at the student. "Can you believe this bigot?" I told my fellow conspirators. This was my answer to anyone who disagreed with me and my ideals. The world was full was racists, bigots, and homophobes who needed to be got rid of. It was my duty to make the world a safer place for all humanity.

I was well-read and smart and knew all about the world and politics. I did not need an ignorant, backward person to contradict my beliefs. How dare she, a person who was brainwashed by her Christian faiths, argue with me? I am an enlightened student of culture and philosophy. I can distinguish right from wrong, and no one has the right to tell me otherwise. Later, I realized how stupid and ignorant I really was.

Alexander Pope stated in "An Essay on Criticism," 1709, "A little learning is a dangerous thing; drink deep or taste not the Pierian spring: there shallow draughts intoxicate the brain and drinking largely sobers us again."

If I had heeded this expression, I would have not been as pigheaded and sure of myself as I was. This feeling of superiority in my intelligence stayed with me for the longest time. No one could argue with me on any topic, because I knew it all, and they were all ignorant idiots who did not know any better. I was so sure of my thought process that I only surrounded myself with individuals who shared my values and ideals. I further distanced myself from my uninformed, backward, and uncultured family and immersed myself with enlightened individuals. I stopped calling home and refused to respond to any of my family's phone calls. In my opinion they were nothing but idiots trying to pull me back to the Dark Ages. I was having none of that. I wanted to be free of all their old-fashioned prehistoric values.

Another incident happened to me in college, which I thought at the time was my crowning glory as a feminist crusader. A lecturer was due to have a talk concerning the deteriorating situation of the Christian minorities in the Middle East. A Syrian Christian and Yazidi women were scheduled to give a testimony of their lives under the Islamic Republic.

I was mad about that. I knew that some racist was going to use these poor, misguided women for their own gain. It was ridiculous to assume that Muslims ill-treat anyone else. When I heard about the lecture, I started making plans to disturb this lecture. In my opinion this lecturer was an instrument that the conservative right was using to hide the West's murder and mayhem in the Middle East. No educated person in my opinion would believe such things. It was the Christians that have invaded these Muslim lands.

Both Bush presidents invaded Islamic countries and toppled their legitimate government. They left the countries they invaded in mayhem. How dare they come here and try to falsify history? I was mad at these privileged, misogynistic, and patriarchal groups trying to act all holy now about some exaggerated incident in the Middle East. This was ridiculous. Everyone knew that white Christian male men were the source of all evil. They enslaved all people of color and destroyed cultures that were much more advanced than they were.

With my comrades in arms, we planned well. We contacted the local Muslim student chapter in our college, and with their help we planned to disturb the lecture. The day of the lecture, we picketed in front of the lecture hall. We chanted slogans against the lecturer and the organizers of the lecture. You should see the faces of these two idiotic women when we showed up. We screamed them down and forced them to leave with their tails behind their legs.

We were not about to let these racist bigots spread their lies and distortion of the truth. We were able to shut down the lecture. This was a triumph for us. We were able to get rid of these despicable people.

Jalal

I met Jalal when I was in my senior year of college. I was a nursing student and had one semester to graduate. I was with a group of friends in the cafeteria, when I looked up and saw a tall, olive-skinned man with dark hair and dark eyes. He had rugged features, a large nose, and a beard. I was mesmerized by his looks. He kept staring at me as if I were the only person in the room. It was love at first sight. I could not tear my eyes from him. He was accompanied by two other students I knew very well. Then Jalal and the students approached our group and introduced Jalal to me.

"Tina," my friend Jamil said, "I would like to introduce you to a friend of ours, Jalal. Jalal is from the Middle East, and he is here to complete his graduate studies."

"Hello, Jalal," I said, "it is genuinely nice to meet you."

I held out my hand to shake his, but Jalal did not shake my hand; he had his hand on his chest and nodded. I was taken aback by his behavior and did not know how to react. I felt like an idiot with my hand extended in the air. Why was he snubbing me? What have I done to offend him? Did my staring at him offend him somehow?

"Salam Aliekoum," Jalal said. "It is an honor to meet you, Tina."

The two students who were with Jalal introduced him to the rest of the group that was with me. I realized that Jalal only shook hands with the boys; the other girls in my group got the same greeting I got. I felt a bit better after I realized that Jalal had not singled me out with his greeting. I was intrigued by this exotic individual and wanted to know everything about him and his ways.

He was extremely courteous toward all females, and I felt he signaled me out for special treatment. He never looked any female directly in the eye. He was always respectful and curious toward all of us. In all my life I never felt so valued and respected by an adult male. He never cursed or said anything demeaning toward any individual.

I was curious about this person, who seemed so different from any individual I have encountered. He never drank alcohol and seemed always respectful toward other people. He did not flirt with any women and kept a respectful distance from them. He spoke in a low and gentle voice and never raised his voice to anyone.

In my view he embodied all that a gentleman ought to be. He never made any snide and insulting remarks toward any woman in his presence. Jalal represented all the attributes of what a man should be. He did not cower before anyone. He stood up for his ideas. He did not care if anyone approved of him or not. I felt protected in his presence. Finally, here was a man who respected me as a woman, did not belittle me, but at the same time was true to himself.

I was fed up with guys who saw me as a ticket to having a good time. I was sick and tired of all the partying going around me. I wanted to feel I belonged somewhere and was part of a society that respected women and did not try to sexualize them. I felt that he was my safe harbor in a vicious storm. How great would it be to be with an individual who respected me treated me like the finest crystal?

All I could see around me was a corrupt and unethical society. Girls were encouraged to have sex as young as thirteen years old. I could see many children born out of wedlock. All guys wanted was to drink and have sex with any available girl out there. Moral values were being discarded by the wayside.

I was looking around for a strong male to look after me. Even though I was a proponent for feminism and equality for the sexes, deep down inside I was attracted to strong and masculine men. I had decried the patriarchy, attacking white men's behavior, and avowing to destroy them. It was something I was brainwashed to believe and regurgitate whenever I was arguing with people concerning male misogyny. It was what I was taught to say.

In my naivety I did not think I was the greatest culprit of all in undermining our society. I had insulted and hurt my parents time after time. I wanted to do what I wanted and would not confirm to my parents' edicts and rules. But now I blamed them for all the ills of society. I was a spoiled brat who did not really know what life was all about.

I was always protected and coddled by my family. They offered the best that life could offer. I wanted for nothing. I was their little princess but did not see it this way. I rejected their love and thought the grass was greener on the other side. They instilled in me good moral values. They taught me how to behave and respect others. My mother taught me how to behave like a lady and respect my body. She told me the any sexual relationship should be within the confines of a loving marriage.

Islam, My Salvation

My fascination with Jalal started me on a journey of my life. I wanted to become a person who Jalal admired and looked at with love and respect. I wanted to marry and create a family with him. I began studying about Islam and how to be a good Muslim. I read a lot of books and joined classes that helped me understand more about Jalal's culture. I had rejected my culture, so I felt bereft and lonely. I had no moral compass to turn to. Jalal filled this moral void in my life.

Bit by bit I began to withdraw from my friends. I refused to go out with my girlfriends and join any activities they were involved in. It became apparent to all who knew me that I was changing before their eyes. I joined a local mosque and started to learn the Quran and the Arabic language. Jalal became my world. I did all this to please him. I felt that I belonged to someone and something.

At the local mosque, my eyes were opened to new and wonderful ideas. I was fascinated with all this new information given to me. I learned the true worth of the human spirit. Islam for me encompassed everything that was right in our world. It was the ultimate answer to all the world's problems.

I did not delve deeply into the mosque's affiliations or teaching. I did not question their teaching or if they were teaching me the true version of Islam. I had little knowledge of the fact that, like any other religion, some sheiks and Imams taught their own version of Islam. They interpreted the holy book according to their own perverted views. The Imams wanted the Quran to serve their purpose, not the other way around.

I did not know how pure and innocent everything was portrayed to be. These preachers taught me so much about the human condition. I was really surprised to learn all the goodness and kindness presented to me. My eyes were opened to a new and beautiful world. Since I could not read Arabic, the teachers at my mosque interpreted the deep meaning of every world in the Quran.

The Muslim civilization gave everything to the world. Music, art, medicine, and architecture. While the Christian world was wallowing in the Dark Ages, Islam was a ray of modernity and advancement. It was the Muslim world that had preserved the arts. The Christians were destroying everything that was contrary to their narrow view of their world. They used barbaric methods to destroy and silence all who opposed them.

I learned that in Islam women were put on a pedestal. Contrary to many ignorant Western thought, women were equal to men in Islam. I was taken aback by this idea. I, a feminist, could relate to that. God respected women so much that he wanted her to wear the hijab to protect her from the eyes of anyone who seeks to do her harm.

"For Muslim men and women, for believing men and women, for devout men and women, for true men and women, for men and women who are patient and constant, for men and women who humble themselves, for men and women who give in charity, for men and women who fast, for men and women who guard their chastity, and for men and women who engage much in Allah's praise, for them has Allah prepared forgiveness and great reward" (Noble Quran 33:35).

According to my teachers, this phrase in the Quran emphasized the equality between men and women. Islam does not discriminate against women but rather gives them equal rights. I loved this idea. The Christian belief demeaned and degraded women. I wanted nothing to do with this faith that was flawed and decimating against women.

Estrangement from Family

As time went by, I isolated myself from all people. I did not want to associate myself with anyone who had an opposing view of my beliefs. I alienated myself from my loved ones, especially my parents and siblings. My parents begged me to see reason and cease on this path of self-destruction. My siblings tried their best to understand my new path in life but asked me to stay within the folds of my family. A family that loved me and would support me no matter what path I decided to travel.

My mother, Jane, on the phone: "Tina, my love, we as your parents love you no matter what you become, but please do not shun us."

"You guys are nothing but infidels who have destroyed my life."

"Tina, we love you and have always wanted what was best for you. We worked hard to give you everything."

"Please stop with your empty speeches, you were selfish and self-centered. You led me on the wrong path all my life. You never loved or cared for me."

"What do you mean we do not love you? Your father and I sacrificed everything for you and your brothers."

"All you cared about was yourselves and the material world around you. You do not know what true sacrifice is. You were so focused on yourselves and material world around you."

"Honey, please, I beg you come home, and we can discuss all this."

"Listen, lady, from this day forth I do not consider you my parents. I have been given more love and support from complete strangers at my mosque. I have found my true self and refuse to be pulled back into this false world of yours. Do not try and contact me again, or I will call the police. I hate both you and your husband. I have found what a true family is, and I fully intend to grasp it before it disappears before my eyes. I have no place in my life for people such as you. I warn you, never get in touch with me again."

"Tina, please listen to me."

"I cannot take any more of your whining."

I slammed the phone down on my mother and vowed to never get into contact with her. I could not believe how happy I was to do that. Finally, I was free to follow the path of truth and justice. I was elated with my newfound freedom. Let them all rot in hell for all I cared. I knew what I am and what I would become.

I refused to get into contact with my parents since that day. Even though they tried their best to try and contact me, I was adamant in my refusal to have any contact with them or any of my relatives. I even went so far as to threaten them with a restraining order if they persisted in trying to contact me.

My brothers decided to intervene and came to visit at my college. I told them to meet me at a local café not far from where I was staying. I refused to let them come to my dormitory and meet me there. When they asked me to meet them at a local restaurant, I flatly refused their suggestion, telling them that I did not eat in place that did not carry halal meat. My brothers tried questioning me on my ideas, but I just shut them out.

"If you guys want to talk to me, it better be on my own terms. I refuse to be manipulated by ignorant people like you guys."

I did not know at the time the love these two brothers of mine had in their hearts for a sister who was both ungrateful and unappreciative of them. They bit their tongues and brushed off my insults to come and meet me. I cry every time I remember how I treated both David and Sam.

Before meeting my brothers, I got in contact with Jalal. I told him about my meeting with my brothers. He was not happy about it. He warned me that I better be stern to them. He did not want me around these infidels.

"I warn you, Tina," Jalal threatened, "if you think I will tolerate any relationship with these people, you can think again. I will cut you off. I am a devoted man and will not have these people influencing my family. Do you understand?"

At the assigned date and time of the meeting, I headed toward the café in downtown Boston. I entered the café, and waiting for me were my two bothers, David and Sam. They both were taken aback by what I was wearing, but this did not deter them from rushing up to me to hug me close. I did not return their hugs and was very standoffish with them.

My brother David: "Tina, please listen to us, we love you and want the best for you. Please do not cut yourself from us your family."

"Do not touch me. Even though you are my blood brothers, you are still males, and I do not want you to touch me."

David begged me: "Tina, please do not say that, you are our beloved sister."

I was not happy with David. "Do not try to undermine me. I know what you guys are and how you operate."

Hurt by my vicious words, David asked me, "What do you mean by that?"

"Look at how you live your life, how you conduct your life."

Sam, in a shocked voice, asked, "Conduct our lives?"

"Yes, look how you drink, date, and sleep around."

David, in a hurt voice, asked, "What does that have to do with the love we have for you, our sister?"

Sam tried reasoning with me: "We never insulted or belittled you."

I scoffed at them: "The way you live your life is an insult to humanity itself. I want to live a just and righteous life, not a life of corruption."

Sam asked, "Who are we hurting with our actions? We do not harm anyone, or force anyone to live our lives."

David tried reasoning with me: "Everyone has the right to choose how to live. We do not want to lose you as a sister. We accept you any way you are, but we do not want to lose you in our lives. Our parents love you. We love you and want you in our lives."

I dismissed them with a shrug. "I do not want you in my life. We are not on the same page in our lives. I do not accept your way of life. You must either change your way, or I will cut you from my life. You guys are nothing but an insult to me. I cannot hold my head up in my adopted community with a family like this. You are not my family anymore. You are all dead to me."

Sam begged me to reconsider my cruel edict: "Please, Tina, be logical here. You cannot cut us out of your lives like this."

David, my brother, pleaded with me: "Tina, we love you."

I stood up and walked away from them. I could see the hurt on both my beloved brothers' faces. They were truly shocked with my actions. I was so full of indignant pride and full of my own worth, that it gave me great pleasure to the hurt on their faces. I wanted to hurt them and alienate them from me. In my blind selfishness I wanted to make them feel worthless and unwanted.

The prophet said in the Quran (5:51): "O you who believe! do not take the Jews and the Christians for friends; they are friends of each other; and whoever amongst you takes them for a friend, then surely he is one of them; surely Allah does not guide the unjust people."

Who was I to question what the prophet deems right? My brothers were infidels. I did not want them to corrupt my way of living. I always found a way to justify my actions.

I felt vindicated by my actions. I considered my family dead to me. They who lived their lives in a desolate way. Everything was permissible for them. Alcohol, sex, divorce, and children outside marriage. Nothing was a taboo anymore. Young teenagers having sex and getting pregnant. Our society was going down the drain before our eyes, and no one was doing anything to stop this downward spiral. The destruction of our society was imminent, and there was no way that that could be stopped. I did not want to bring up my children in such a desolate and corrupt place. I wanted my children to grow up respecting women, their bodies, their families, and each other.

If I were a bit aware of the hypocrisy of the matter, I would not have been so proud of myself or my actions. I was such a staunch feminist raging against the injustices of the world, calling for free love and equality between all sexes. Yet here I was advocating a way of life that was vastly different from what I had preached previously. I justified my actions with the feminist explanation that it is a women's choice to live any way she wanted. She was the one to chose the way she wanted to lead her life. Wearing the hijab was liberating. It empowered me as a woman.

From that day forth I refused to have anything to do with my family. I cut them from me like a useless limp. I was happy with my decision; I had my own adopted family and soon would marry the love of my life, Jalal. My stupidity was going to cost me big time. Unbeknownst to me, something happened that would derail my future for a long time. We will revisit this episode in my life later on.

Isolation

The story of my journey with Jalal started with such purity and love. For the first time in my life, I felt valued and appreciated. I was not a sexualized being but rather a respected person worthy to be a wife and a mother. He taught many things about his religion and culture that I found fascinating. He wanted to marry me and start a family with me. He cautioned beforehand that I needed to convert to Islam and learn about his culture before he could marry me. He wanted a pious Muslim girl for his wife. A wife that would establish a devout Muslim family with him.

Jalal always insisted on having a woman chaperone with me when we talked. This woman was his sister Khadija. Khadija watched me like a hawk and reported all my action to Jalal. Khadija was to accompany me wherever I went. Jalal wanted a chaste woman as his wife. It was unseemly of me to be seen without a chaperone. It might seem strange to some people, but I accepted all his edicts without a word.

He made his wishes noticeably clear on how our courtship should be conducted. We never touched or sat close to each other. He averted his eyes from me. He did it out of respect for me as a woman. I was flattered by his actions. He asked me to dress in a more conservative mood. He explained that he did not want other men to see my beauty. A women's beauty was for her husband alone. We talked for hours each day, and I was slowly getting caught in his web.

Jalal asked me to stop socializing with any of my friends. He specifically asked me to stop talking to any of my male friends. In his opinion, a chaste woman did not talk to men who were not related to her. Jalal stressed the fact that he wanted to marry a chaste woman. He asked me to segregate myself from any males during my lectures at college. Me, the raging feminist, did not see anything wrong in this.

In one of our conversations, in a voice full of authority, Jalal told me: "Tina, you need to sit in the back of the classroom and not next to any males. If a male sat next to you, get up from your seat and move to another seat."

I did not understand him at first and asked him in a joking manner, "Jalal, is that not extreme in your opinion? I am not talking to these guys. I am just sitting in class and listening to the lecture."

Jalal looked shook his head at me and explained in a voice one uses with a child, "Tina, since you are still foreign to our culture and religion, you need to let me tell you what is best for you."

Listening to Jalal, I felt that he genuinely cared and loved me to take the time to explain these important things to me. He wanted me to be fully integrated into his culture. A true feeling of belonging spread throughout my body. He was taking the time to explain these things to me, an ignorant American.

In a superior voice, Jalal explained to me: "When a male who is not related to you sits next to you, he might be overcome with lustful thoughts and act on them. I do not want any wife of mine to be lusted after by any man. Women should stay pure of heart and pure of body."

In my typical argumentative manner, I asked him, "But is that not the other man's problem? I did not do anything to cause any such lustful thoughts."

In a condescending manner, Jalal for the first time looked me straight in the eye and said, "It is the duty of every chaste and honorable woman to conduct herself in such a way as to be invisible to others in the society, especially the males. Do you understand what I am saying to you? I do not want a wife who flaunts herself in front of other men. It is unseemly behavior, and this I would not tolerate."

I was scared by his manner and was afraid he would turn against me. In a timid and conciliatory voice I replied: "I understand, Jalal."

Jalal turned his face away from me and continued: "Tina, you need to accept our ways if you want to be part of my life. I do not condone any action from my wife that is contrary to the teachings of Islam."

I wanted to appease him and replied, "I know, Jalal, but give me time to understand and learn more about it."

Jalal was not easily appeased by my manner and wanted to stress his point: "If you genuinely cared about me, you need to accept all that I am. I will not accept anything less than an ideal wife in my life."

I was truly repentant and wanted to make sure he knew it: "I promise I will do my best."

Jalal looked at Khadija and told me in an offhanded manner: "See that you do. I will not accept anything less."

Jalal stood up to leave, hesitated for a minute, and then turned around and said: "Tina, you need to start wearing the hijab. I will not be seen with you anymore if you do not at least cover your hair."

"But why?" I asked.

"I told you, Tina, I will not commit myself to a woman who flaunts herself before other men."

"But, Jalal, I am dressing in a very conservative manner. I show no skin whatsoever."

"It does not matter, Tina. I do not want any man to see your uncovered hair. I am ashamed that other men look at you with lust in their eyes. If you care for me, you need to adhere to what I feel is best."

Jalal further explained to me: "According to Imam Shahid Mehdi, a great Islamic leader, women are not entitled to respect when they walk around without a hijab. They are to blame for it when they are attacked. All crimes that occur against women is because they are not covered. When they are not covered, you have no respect for them."

I looked at Jalal and asked, "Does the Quran state that?"

"Yes, it does. Imam Shahid Mehdi further elaborated on this matter by saying, 'She disobeys her master, there are two places in the Qur'an has ordered her to cover themselves… Women make a clean

34

society dirty when they walk around without a hijab. They are not entitled to respect and are not valuable as those who wear a hijab.'"

Fearing disappointing him, I readily agreed to his edict: "Yes, Jalal."

Jalal nodding at Khadija, saying, "Good, Tina. Khadija, my beloved sister, will teach you how to wear the hijab. You need to listen to her and let her guide you. She is well versed in our religion, and I trust her implicitly. She is a chaste woman who knows her limits in life."

In a voice full of admiration, he further added, "Look at how she dresses and avoids all contact with men. She is covered from head to toe. She would not dream of arguing with a man. Try to emulate her actions. She will not lead you on the wrong path, believe me. I have instructed her to be your guide and mentor. Do you understand? You need to respect her. She is very precious to me, and I will not tolerate any disrespect toward her."

After his speech, Jalal stood up and walked away. Khadija nodded her head in agreement.

In a shrill voice, Khadija said, "Listen, Tina, Jalal can have any women he wants, but he chooses you. You need to abide by his wishes. He is greatly honoring you with his attention. Do you even understand the great honor he is bestowing upon you by explaining all these things to you?"

Why was Khadija saying this stuff to me? I knew Jalal was a great guy, but why was she attacking me? "What do you mean?"

Khadija was not to be stopped. "Jalal is very patient and understanding of your needs. He is going out of his way to understand your ignorant Western ways. He is explaining things to you that a child should know."

She bent her head, trying to contain her emotions, adding, "Any good Muslim girl of our culture would know this stuff. Why did he have to fall for a Westerner like you, I do not understand. There are so many good, devoted Muslim girls out there who would be honored to have him as their husband. I can understand his desire for you. Any man would be inflamed by your sexual manner."

"What do you mean by my flaunting myself?" I asked her in a bewildered voice. "I have never sexually flaunted myself to anyone."

"Look at you with your uncovered hair and face." She said, "Uncovered hair incites a man to lust after women. It is up to the woman to protect herself and her honor. If I flaunted myself in front of any man the way you do, my father would have slit my throat."

She continued, "Do you truly. I cannot see why he wants to be with you, when all you do is argue with him. I wish he never laid eyes upon you. You lured him with you lustful and deceitful Western ways, and now he is hooked."

"Why are you saying that, Khadija? I thought you were my friend."

"Me your friend. You must be joking. I can never befriend a woman such as you. A devoted Muslim women such as me does not have an infidel whore for a friend."

I was deeply hurt by her attack. In a hurt voice I asked her, "What have I ever done to you? Why are you talking to me like that? I love Jalal and want to do everything in my power to please him. Do you not want a wife that loves your brother with all her heart? I will always be faithful to him."

Khadija scoffed at me. In a voice filled with hurt and outrage, she said, "Do you? The greatest honor anyone can have in this life is to convert to Islam. Are you ready for that? Are you ready to give up your life to become a true follower of Islam? To become a true spouse to Jalal and never question him. The men are the head of the household, and he knows what is best for his family. You need to support him in all his endeavors."

"I am more than willing. I will do anything for Jalal. He is my one true love. I have given up everything to be with him."

Khadija, knowing that she could not argue further, said, "Good. Tomorrow we will go to the mosque to start your conversion process. You need to listen and accept everything without any question. Do you understand?"

"Yes, I do."

Khadija, My Mentor

Khadija, his sister, was my mentor, and she was the one that guided me through the whole process. I had to study the Quran in depth. To understand and read the Quran, I had to learn the read and write Arabic. It was a long and tedious process. I did not get any breaks. Khadija was a hard taskmaster. She made me study for hours on end. She refused to speak any English to me. I had to work extremely hard to learn the language.

I moved in with her and Jalal's widowed mother. Khadija, I was told, was a widow with three children to take care of. Two girls and a boy. Hammoudi, Rima, and Sahar. I helped around the house and with her small children. I cleaned, cooked, and took care of the children. She and her mother were refugees from Iraq. As refugees, they were entitled to many benefits from the American government. They received free housing and welfare benefits. I also found out that Jalal was registered refugee. He had accompanied his mother and sister to the States.

From the stories they told me, I understood they had to flee from Iraq due to the persecution they were enduring under then new Shia regime. They said that they were harassed and persecuted. They explained how, due to the American intervention, they were forced to leave their beloved country.

Jalal was continually active within his community. He was always seeking financial help for others like him back in his home country of Iraq. He attended Mosque every day, giving speeches, and asking for donations to help his brethren back in Iraq. He also traveled back and forth to Iraq.

I was so proud of Jalal. He was a true hero in my eyes. He worked hard to help others. He was also a great spokesperson for his oppressed people. He had an unwavering support for his cause. He was the voice for the voiceless. I put him on a pedestal. I never stopped to question his actions. I was his complete captive.

I felt that Khadija resented me. I could not understand why she would feel this hatred toward me. Did she feel I was taking her brother's attention from her and her children? I knew she was a widow and wholly dependent on her brother for support. I kept wondering why her deceased husband's family was not involved with her kids' upbringing. She always put me down and insulted me anytime she got the chance. Her hatred was evident for all to see. She never let me forget that I was nothing but an interloper to her family. I could understand her wanting her brother's affection, but she was going overboard. Her jealousy was taking a vindictive streak.

When I brought up her behavior to Jalal, he was dismissive of my fears. He thought I was imagining things.

"Look, Tina, I am sick and tired of your nagging. You need to understand that my family comes first. You are marrying into a tight-knit family, not an American family where individual do not care about each other. Do not try and come between Khadija and I, you will regret it. I will choose her over you any day. She is special to me, and you need to understand that."

"Jalal," I cried in frustration, "I am not trying to come between you two. I want her to stop insulting and belittling me. I am doing my best to fit in, and she is making it difficult for me. You know how much I love you."

"I know, Tina, I understand that you are going through a lot. Try to understand where she is coming from. She loves me a lot and wants what is best for me. She does not think that you can acclimate to our customs and way of life. You will win her in time."

"Okay, Jalal, I understand. I will try to do my best."

Conversion

The next day, accompanied by Khadija and Sara, I went to the mosque to begin my faith journey into Islam. On our way there, Khadija had a lot to say to me concerning my conversation with Jalal.

"How dare you."

"What did I do now?" I asked her baffled by her unprovoked attack.

"You go telling tales to Jalal."

"What tales?"

"You are lying, bitch. I had to endure a lecture on how to treat you. I am warning you from now on, do not mess with me. You do not know what you are getting yourself in. I can barely tolerate you. If you are not incredibly careful, I can make your life a living hell."

"What have I ever done to you? You treat me as if I am your enemy. Could we not bury the hatchet and be friends? After all, I am going to marry your brother."

When I looked at Khadija's face, I could see pain reflected in her eyes. It was as if I had pierced her heart with a lance. What crime had I committed? Why did my upcoming marriage to her brother give me such pain? Was I such a bad person that I was not worthy of such an honor?

I knew that Khadija had a close relationship with Jalal, but this really was strange. Looking at her face, I felt as if I were an adulterer stealing someone's husband. It was an absurd feeling. Why would that even enter my mind? I knew that Khadija feared that Jalal will ignore his responsibilities toward her and her children if he married me.

I tried reassuring her of my commitment to her and her family. "Khadija, believe me, my dear, I will never come between you and your brother. Your children will always have a special place in my heart, I promise you that. Jalal loves you and would never abandon you."

"You say that now," she scoffed at me, "but we all know that a man forgets his obligations once he is in bed with a new wife."

"What do you mean new wife?" I asked. "I am his first and only wife."

Khadija looked at me with absolute derision. "You do know that Jalal can marry four wives. Polygamy is an accepted practice in our religion."

I looked at her as if she had lost her mind. "That might be so, but polygamy is illegal in the States. Jalal loves me, and he would not stoop to marrying another woman."

Khadija smiled at me and nodded her head. I felt she wanted to tell me something but thought better of it. It was a bit frustrating not able to establish a good relationship with Jalal's sister. I wanted her to like me. I felt that, given a chance, we could be great friends. I wanted to become a part of his family so much that I put up with all the abuse. I felt that things would eventually get better, and they would accept me as one of them.

When we arrived, we were met by the sheikh at the mosque who asked me to repeat the Shahada three times.

"Repeat after me, three times the following, *La illah illa allah was Mohammad rasulla allah.* There is one God and Mohammad is the Prophet of God."

"La Illaha illa Allah was Mohammad Rasoula Allah, La Illaha illa Allah was Mohammad Rasoula Allah, La Illaha illa Allah was Mohammad Rasoula Allah."

After I said the Shahada three times, I was proclaimed a Muslim. I was amazed by how fast it took. I was so proud of myself. The women then took me aside and put the hijab on my head. Finally, I had converted to Islam, and Jalal was going to be so proud of me.

The following days, I went back to the mosque to start studying the Quran and learning the Arabic language. It was difficult at first because the Arabic language was difficult and completely foreign. I had to learn a different alphabet. It was not easy, but my love for Jalal made me persevere in my efforts to continue in my quest.

I became a prisoner of my own thirst to please a man who would become my husband. As the days passed by, I became more and more steeped into my own world, disregarding anything that was outside the realm of this isolated environment I had surrounded myself in. I dropped out of college, and lost contact with everyone from my previous world. I studied day and night to become fluent in Arabic and well versed in the Quran.

I was so proud of myself and the progress I made. The more I learned, the closer I felt with Jalal. His world became my world, and his word became law. I became blinded to any of Jalal's faults. I saw his controlling and domineering personality as a positive trade. He was protecting me from the outside world. His love for me was so great that he did not want to share me with the outside world. I was like a precious diamond in his eyes. I was told that if you have a diamond, you do not throw it in front of pigs to trample on. His love for his family was wonderful. He treated his nephews and nieces as if they were his own children. How could I not love such a man?

I saw little of Jalal through this whole process. He was traveling back and forth to his home country. One day, Jalal arrived home, and he automatically sought Khadija out. They disappeared into her bedroom and did not emerge all day long. His mother did not even blink an eye concerning this strange behavior. Later, I asked Jalal, why had he not sought me out?

Jalal replied that it was forbidden for a male and female not related to be in each other's company without a proper chaperone. He further stressed that he was respecting me as his future wife by keeping his distance.

Khadija was on cloud nine after that day. She seemed extremely happy even though I still felt her resentment toward me. I kept wondering to myself, why would Jalal spend the whole day sequestered with his sister in her bedroom? When I asked him, he said that they were discussing family issues that had arisen back in their home country. Issues that I could not understand or help them solve. In my naive way I accepted his explanation as gospel.

Aisha Is Born

One day Khadija asked me to change my name because in her opinion it was a holdout of my Western roots.

"Tina, I think you need to change your name."

"Why?"

"It is an infidel, Christian name, and it offends many people."

"How can a simple name offend people?"

"Tina is short for Christiana, and that stands for Christ. As you know we do not believe in Christ as the son of God, but rather a prophet of God. When a true Muslim hears your name, he or she will think that you are not a true Muslim."

"It is just a name. I do not think anyone will be offended by it."

"Tina, how many times do I have to tell you that you need to obey without question? I have taken you, a pathetic, ignorant American into my house and this is the way you repay me. You question my judgment." She took a deep breath, agitated by my questioning.

She looked at me with utter contempt, saying in a spiteful voice, "Jalal has assigned me this thankless act of seeing to your welfare, and all I get is this attitude from you. Let me tell you that I would not put up with it. Do not question me again, you stupid whore. Whose side do you think my brother would take if things come to pass?"

I was taken aback by this personal attack. I have done all they asked for. I moved in with Khadija to learn from her to be a perfect Muslim woman. I catered to her and her children. I cooked, cleaned, and took care of her mother. I also applied to social welfare and gave my welfare benefits to her to spend as she saw fit. I obeyed her every dictate, so why was she attacking me so viciously? I was so scared that Jalal would turn against me that I would have done anything to appease her. I had learned a hard lesson that Khadija had much sway with Jalal. I did not want to rock the boat and upset her.

With a heavy heart, I agreed to her demand. "I am sorry, Khadija, I will change my name."

"Good, I talked it over with my brother, and he says that he wants to call you Aisha, after our prophet's wife. Aisha was the prophet's most beloved wife. She is a woman all girls aspire to become like. She was an obedient follower of our great prophet. She never questioned him. Her father, Omar Abu Bakr, a follower of our great prophet, and the first of the great caliph to rule over the Islamic nation."

"Aisha."

"Yes, Jalal is showing you great honor by choosing this name for you. He also wants me to prepare for your wedding."

When I heard that little tidbit of information, I got so excited. Finally, I was going to marry the man I love above all else.

"Where is Jalal now? I have not seen him for a while."

She looked at me with utter hatred and replied, "Jalal had to go back home and visit family. You know how family oriented we are. He has obligations back home that he cannot shrug. You need to understand the world does not in any shape or form revolve around you. When Jalal has finished his duties, he will come back here. Do you understand?"

"Yes, I know, but he is constantly traveling. I miss him a lot."

"Aisha, you would learn to never question your husband in the future. He cannot cater to your every whim. You are being selfish and ignorant when you question him. My brother is an honorable man. He promised to marry you, and he will. Even though my mother and I disapprove of you and your ways."

Khadija was on a roll: "You know how much good work Jalal does. As you sit feeling sorry for yourself like a spoiled brat, he is risking his life helping our people back home. You only think of yourself."

I was taken aback by this statement. Why would they disapprove of me? I have done everything within my power to please them. Why was Khadija constantly belittling me? What have I done to earn her ire? Well, I thought to myself, it does not matter because I know Jalal loved me and would make me very happy when we got married.

The following day, Khadija and her mother called me to come to the sitting room. Usually, they never invited me to sit with them. I felt that I was making headway with my new in-laws.

"Aisha," Khadija said, "come and sit down with us. We have something to discuss with you."

I was so happy they had invited me to join them that I automatically replied, "Yes, of course, whatever you want."

I sat down on the couch across from Khadija and her mother, looking expectantly at them. I thought that they were going to let me know when Jalal was coming to visit to set up the wedding date.

"My brother got in touch with me and asked me to set up your wedding for next week."

"That is great, I cannot wait for this joyous occasion to happen."

Khadija looked at me with a frown marring her face, "Yes, I know how excited you are, but Jalal has put a condition for the marriage to go forth."

I was a bit shocked by this piece of news. "What do you mean by that?"

"Jalal asks you to wear the niqab before he would marry you. He refuses to marry a woman who shows her face to other man."

In shock, I asked, "But I thought the niqab was not part of Islam?"

In a shrill voice, Khadija answered me, "Do not lecture me on what Islam is, you ignorant idiot. I am sick and tired of your resistance to change. Can you not see what a great honor Jalal is doing you? He is willing to marry an American girl and to enlighten her on the true path of the Islamic faith. He has saved your life."

She took a deep breath and continued her tirade. "Your life was going to waste before he picked you up from the trash. I cannot believe you would question this. Do you think I would wear the niqab if it were not required in our religion? Do you understand me, you disgusting creature"?

I looked at her, beseeching, "This is difficult for me. I understand why I need to wear the hijab, but the niqab is it not too much."

Not able to contain her fury, Khadija continued her lecture. "Listen to me, you idiot, you have no choice. You either wear the niqab, or the marriage is off. I wear the niqab. Do you think you are better than me?"

In a shaking voice, I replied honestly, "I understand what you are saying and would willing wear the niqab, if that is what Jalal wants."

Khadija uttered a sigh of relief. "Good, then it is settled. You will marry Jalal next Friday at the mosque. We will meet him there. He refuses to see you before that. He will move here with us after the marriage. You will have your own room. I warn you, Aisha, you need to learn obedience and self-control. My brother would not tolerate such behavior."

"Yes, Khadija," I replied in a subdued voice.

All this time Jalal's mother looked on our discussion without uttering any word. She rarely ever spoke to me. It was strange how she looked right through me as if I did not exist. I was convinced that once I marry her son and show how much I loved him, she would come around. After all, she loved her son, and I was positive that she would eventually accept me as her daughter-in-law. I would prove myself to her and Khadija.

I did not want to heed her warning. I knew Jalal loved me and would put me above all else. I knew the man I loved, and he would not tolerate any abuse toward me. I have given everything to be with this man. He was my life. I was going to establish a family with him. I started to imagine the family I would have with him. A dark-eyed, olive-skinned boy who looked like Jalal and a blue-eyed, blond girl who looked like me.

I started to wear the full Muslim garb. Nothing of me showed, even my eyes. It did not faze me much because I felt I was doing the right thing. My life was going in the right direction. I was not allowed to go out in public much. If I left the house, Khadija always accompanied me. I was a virtual prisoner but did not see it that way. I felt content and happy. Next Friday could not come fast enough for me.

Marriage

The following Friday, I went to the mosque accompanied by a scowling Khadija. I was garbed from head to foot in black. I looked like a bag of coal, but I felt beautiful. I was so excited; finally, I was going to marry Jalal. When I got there, all us women were segregated form the men. I saw Jalal talk to the Imam, who had informed him of my arrival. The ceremony took place between Jalal and the Imam. The Imam had beforehand asked me if I wanted to marry Jalal. I automatically gave my consent. Finally, I was a married woman. I belonged to someone.

Khadija did not smile once throughout the whole ceremony. She was upset and cried throughout the ceremony. She looked as if she were attending a funeral rather than a wedding.

After the ceremony, Jalal escorted me out of the mosque and took me straight home to his sister and mother's home. I was taken aback a bit. I thought we were going to go somewhere else for a while to spend time alone together. I did not say anything because I thought he wanted to start our marriage life with his mother's blessing. Umm Jalal was happy to see her son. She hugged and kissed him but made no such overtures toward me. After receiving his mother's blessing, he dragged me to my room to consummate the marriage.

This was the time my nightmare of a life began. With my heart filled with love and longing, I expected this night to be the best experience of my life. How wrong I was. Jalal shut the bedroom door behind us, threw me on the bed, and fell on me. He was not gentle or showed any compassion toward me.

Jalal's Nephew and Nieces

Jalal made extra effort to be with his nephew and nieces. He spent a lot of times with them. They kept calling him "Baba," which means father in Arabic. I thought that was very touching. These kids looked at their uncle as if he was their father. They were remarkably close to him. Khadija's children did not feel the same way toward me. They never listened to me and were always there to throw insults to my face. I tried awfully hard to be nice to them, but they had picked on their mother's disrespect for me and took their cue from her.

When I tried discussing their behavior toward me to Jalal, he scoffed at me, saying I was imagining things.

"Jalal, they call me whore instead of Khalto [*auntie* in Arabic]. It hurts me when they keep insulting me. I beg you to tell them to show me some respect."

"Do not be overdramatic, Aisha. I am sure you must have misheard what they said. They are very respectful children and would not use such words. They just need to get used to you."

I tried to take Jalal's words to heart and worked extremely hard trying to establish a relationship with Khadija's children. I took care of them, washed their clothes, cleaned their rooms, and cooked their food. I also helped them with their homework. All this did not change their view of me. They still resented me. They made fun of me, spat at me, and insulted me to my face. These kids were out of control. They had no respect toward me as their uncle's wife.

I begged Jalal to talk to them. He did not want to get involved. He said that he thought I was blowing things out of proportion. They behaved like angels in front of him, but the minute he turned his back, they were back to their antics. It was my word against mine, and he always took their side of the story.

These kids could do no wrong in his eyes. He treated them as if they were his own children. He always gave preferential treatment toward the boy. He ignored the girls most of the time. The boy ruled the roost. He hit his sisters and belittled them. When I told Khadija I was concerned about his behavior, she scoffed at my concerns, telling me to mind my own business. It was very strange how attached these kids were to my husband. You would think that he was their father. They doted on him and listened to him. He was their hero. He spent more time with them than he did with me, his wife.

Pregnant

Jalal had been nice to me for a while. He had been treating me well and took care of my every need. He was even gentle with me in the bedroom. For the first time in my marriage, I felt satisfaction in my marriage bed. He had stopped abusing me. He even made his sister, Khadija, and her children stop harassing me. I was on cloud nine. This was the Jalal I had fallen in love with. Both his mother and sister seemed to have accepted me as part of the family and as Jalal's wife. What more could I ask for?

After I got pregnant with my child, Jalal told me it was time we visited his homeland. He wanted his child to be born in his homeland and exposed to his culture and religion. I was not convinced of going there, but Jalal convinced me that it was the best course of action.

I was terrified of traveling to Iraq. I have watched the news and knew that it was a war zone. I also felt that it would not have the proper medical facilities if something went wrong with my pregnancy. I was still not convinced it was the best course of action.

"Listen, Aisha it is only going to be for a couple of weeks. I want you to meet my extended family. You know how important family is to us."

"Jalal, I am a bit hesitant to travel while pregnant. I do not want to travel to a place where I do not know what medical treatment they have in your home country." I took a deep breath and continued with my argument, "I am terrified of going to a war zone country. What would happen to us? What if we were kidnapped or caught between two warring parties?"

"Aisha, my home country is not as savage as you believe. What you see in the media does not reflect the reality of life in my home country."

He took a deep breath and continued in this vein: "We have some of the best medical personal and best doctors. They are trained to be doctors according to the Sharia."

I was still afraid of the unknown. It did not seem logical to me to go to a country where people have been fighting each other. Seeing the fear reflected in my eyes, Jalal looked at me and smiled.

"Aisha, do you not trust me?"

I looked at him and smiled. I loved this man so much. He was my world. "Of course, I trust you. I married you and gave up everything to be with you. I love you with all my heart. But you yourself are a refugee. You escaped from the horror of persecution. Why would you want to take your family back to this horrible palace to visit?"

"Sometimes, Aisha, I doubt your so-called love for me. You know I protect what is mine. Since you and the baby are mine, I will always protect you. Do you think I will take my family to a place where they might be harmed? Things have improved drastically since I left. Our people are getting stronger, and we are taking control of the situation."

I could not counter his argument, so I kept quiet, but I was not convinced of his argument.

Jalal did not push it further. It seemed he had planted the seed of traveling to his homeland in my head.

I felt as if my pregnancy had bound us together as a couple. Jalal was ecstatic when he found out I carried his child and heir. He strutted around, and his joy was evident for all to see. I was blind to all but the joy I felt during that period.

Khadija, the Widow

Khadija, his sister, was greatly subdued during this time. Even though she stopped her harassment, I felt she was not happy about the whole situation. I caught her crying a couple of times. Sometimes I saw Jalal trying to console her. They would disappear into her bedroom for hours on end, and she would emerge more cheerful, but I could still see the misery in her eyes.

I kept wondering if she missed her deceased husband and felt a bit of jealousy of the relationship Jalal and I had. In my own way I felt sorry for her situation. I wanted to do something special for her. Since I was a good Muslim wife, I tried talking to Jalal about it.

After one of intimate times in the bedroom, the only time we had any privacy, I asked Jalal, "Jalal, what was Khadija's husband like?"

I could see that Jalal was shocked by my question. He could barely get a word out. Fearing I had upset him, I quickly added, "The only reason I ask this question, is because I feel Khadija seems sad all the time." I took a deep breath, trying to gather my courage, and continued, "I know you love your nephew and nieces like your own, and treat Khadija well, but I believe that Khadija needs to find a husband for herself. Her children need to feel secure, and maybe by providing her with a husband, they will have a father who will love them and take care of them."

Jalal jumped off our bed and started screaming and throwing insults at me.

"You conniving bitch!" he screamed at me, his beautiful features contorted in an ugly fashion. "What are you trying to do? Break my family apart? Do you think just because you are my wife and I treat you well, I will do what you want?" Taking a deep breath, he tried to calm down.

"Jalal!" I screamed at him for the first time in my life. "Calm down. You are going to have a stroke."

"I cannot believe you ask me to calm down after what you said."

I looked at him, perplexed by his reaction to my suggestion.

"What did I say that was so wrong? Khadija is a beautiful young widow. Her life should not be over just because her husband died. I am not trying to harm her or break up your family. I know you love your sister and her children. I just want what is best for her and her children."

"Aisha, just shut up and do not ever raise your voice to me again. No wife of mine will talk to me in this manner. Do you understand me? I am your husband, and you need to show me the respect due to me. No true Muslim woman will dare raise her voice to me. You need to understand that. Your Western upbringing stills shines through. I will not tolerate such behavior."

Smiling at him to calm him down, I said, "I am sorry if I upset you, my love, I just wanted what was best for her."

Shaking his head in shock, Jalal looked at me with a disdainful manner. I could see he was trying to control himself and said, "Listen to me, Aisha, you might be my wife, but you are not to get involved in such a matter."

Why was Jalal acting in this manner? I thought he was overreacting. I was only suggesting, not trying to start World War III. What was wrong with him? He seemed to be taking it personally. As if I were suggesting he cast his sister and children aside. But it seemed that Jalal had been insulted with my suggestion. I was still sitting on the bed. He lunged at me and imprisoned me under him. He looked me in the eyes and in a very calm voice said, "Aisha, I want you to listen to me very carefully. Khadija is very precious to me, and she is the second most important woman in my life after my mother. You might be my wife, but I will choose Khadija over you any time."

I could not believe my ears. Had Jalal just said what I heard he said? His sister was more important than his wife, the mother of his unborn child. I felt as if a spear had pierced my heart. The man I loved was treating me like an interloper.

I forcibly pushed him away from me and lunged at him, hitting him with my fists. "Do not ever come near me, you jerk, stay away from me. I have taken all I can from you. I will not sit here and hear you say such things to me. Do you hear me? I am your wife. The woman who is expecting your firstborn child, not your mistress."

Jalal had not expected such a reaction from me. I had been such a docile wife. I had never disobeyed him or showed him any disrespect. He did not know what to do. I felt that my pregnancy had made me stronger and that Jalal would see things my way.

Jalal stormed out of our bedroom and left our house. Before leaving, he locked me in my room. The room did not have a telephone, and I was forbidden to carry a mobile phone. I sat on my bed and stewed in silence. I was not going to put up with such behavior. I did want to be treated as a cherished wife, not a sexual object. After a couple of hours, the door to my bedroom opened, and Jalal entered. He looked me in the eyes and smiled. My heart melted when I saw his beautiful face. He was such a handsome man. I loved him so much. I did not want to lose him, but I had my pride. He seemed to be in a consolatory mood.

"Aisha, you know how much I care for you. Please, we do not need to talk about these subjects. We need to concentrate on more important things. Please, I beg you, do not get involved in Khadija's situations. There are certain aspects in her life you do not know about."

Treating Me Well

After this episode, things got a lot better between us. He treated me well, but there were still things that kept nagging at me. Why would he be so defensive toward his sister? Why would he take his sister's children's side against mine? There were many things I did not understand about this family. It puzzled me greatly, but I buried my doubts and refused to question these doubts. I was happy with my lot and did not want to rock the boat.

In addition to this, I did not want to admit to myself or to the world at large that I have committed a mistake by marrying Jalal. I had my pride and did not want my family and friends to tell me, "I told you so." I had burned my bridges behind me.

Jalal's good treatment continued. I did not know at the time that he had an underlying reason to treat me well. He wanted to convince me to travel to Mosul in Iraq with him. He was nice about it. He used all his charm, using my weak points to help me make this momentous decision.

Jalal knew that I still had rights here in the United States. He knew that my rights were protected here. Back in Mosul, I would be under his mercy. I would be dependent on him for my survival. It took some time, but after my six months of pregnancy, I gave Jalal my consent to travel to Mosul. I told him that after the birth of our child, I would travel with the family to Mosul. I gave him my word and told him that I would not go back on my word.

I knew that Jalal wanted me to meet his extended family. He wanted his child to be seeped into his culture and family. He missed them and missed his way of life. He came to the States to get an education, but deep down he never became part of the American culture. He met me an American girl, fell in love, and got married. It was not easy for him to admit his needs to bind with people of his culture and religion. I understood all this and wanted to ease his needs. I loved him so much. The only thing I asked him was to wait until our child was born.

Poor Khadija

During all that, I felt Khadija was greatly subdued. She did not look well and was gaining weight. I was worried about it and fearing she might resent my asking her, asking Jalal about her. Her condition became evident when I was eight months pregnant. We were along in the bedroom, and I took the opportunity to ask. Jalal looked at me in a strange manner and asked, "Why do you ask me about Khadija?"

Jalal being so close to Khadija, I was surprised he had not seen her condition.

"I am just worried about her," I said. "She looks pale and sick most of the time. She has also gained some weight."

Jalal was a bit lost for words. He did not look me in the eye. I felt he was hiding something from me.

"Jalal," I asked, "what is going on? Is Khadija okay?"

"Do you really care, Aishia, about Khadija?"

"What a question Jalal. Of course I care. She is your sister. I love you, and no matter our difference I still respect and love her."

Jalal did not answer me directly. He just kept staring at the wall. I felt he was thinking deeply about the matter. He was weighing his words carefully.

"Okay, Aisha, Khadija is passing through a difficult time in her life. She is taking some prescription medication that causes her to gain weight. Do not worry about it. She is missing her family in Iraq and wants to go back. She is being very patient, and I asked her to wait until you gave birth. This is so we can all travel together."

I felt bad about that. Poor Khadija, she had to wait for me to give birth before visiting her country and family. I also felt grateful for her. She was staying here until I give birth.

I could not wait to give birth to my child. It was a great time for me. Jalal was being courteous and kind. His family seemed to have accepted me, and I was going to visit his homeland. I was also going to be introduced to his extended family. I was so happy. I was feeling I belonged to someone at last. I had a family that really cared for me.

My Daughter Is Born

My due date arrived with no fuss. I was taken to the hospital and delivered a healthy, beautiful baby girl that Jalal and I named Amira. Jalal insisted that no male attend my birth. I had a female doctor and female medical staff. He refused to enter the birthing room with me. Instead, his mother and sister Khadija were present. I thanked God that it was an easy birth.

At first, I felt Jalal was not thrilled that I had delivered a baby girl. He seemed upset, but I thought that it was all in my mind. My daughter was a bundle of joy. How could anyone not love her? I was convinced that Khadija and my mother-in-law were going to make a great fuss out of her. She was after all Jalal's first child. To my utter shock this was not the case. Both Khadija and my mother-in-law did not even give her the time of day. It was as if she was never born. They grumbled about the fact that she cried a lot.

Khadija seemed happy that I did not bare Jalal a son. I heard her muttering to my mother-in-law that my power over Jalal was weaning because I did not present him with a son. I smiled to myself and thought that was utter nonsense. What does the gender of the child I bore have anything to do with Jalal's love for me? Little did I know that Jalal was praying for a son. He wanted a son to carry his name.

When my parents found out that I had given birth to their first grandchild, they tried getting in touch with me. They wanted to see her and make sure that we were doing well. I refused to talk to them, and even threatened them with legal action if they got in touch with me again. I did not want their negative vibes to mar my perfect marriage. I had decided that my daughter would not be exposed to these horrible infidels.

Defending the Freedom Fighters

After the birth of my daughter, Amira, I felt that Jalal had become more insistent on traveling back to Iraq. He was adamant that I set a date. He told me how the Sunni freedom fighters would soon take over Mosul. He was so proud of them. He claimed that the news here in the United States had been trying to blacken the reputation of these freedom fighters.

He told me how he got in touch with some of his relatives and that they were so happy that they were finally going to be free from the oppressive Iraqi government.

I complied with his wishes, and when my beautiful daughter turned a month old, we boarded a plane to take us to Mosul in Iraq.

Since I had never been outside the United States, I felt this was a great adventure. I wanted to learn all I could about the history and culture of Iraq. Toward this end, I started searching the internet for information. I learned a lot by searching the internet. Mosul was a culturally diverse city. The population consists of Arabs, Assyrians, Iraqi Turkmen, and Kurds. I was fascinated by all this information. I could not believe the trove of information on this great city. There were so many historical places that have stood the test of time. There were museums housing these great civilizations.

When I looked up all this information, I felt such joy and relief that my views and my chosen path in life were vindicated. Here was a Muslim country where other religions and cultures thrived. This was positive proof that Islam was a religion of love and tolerance. I wanted to shout out to the naysayers out there to stop attacking my religion and look at the facts. I was really upset by some Middle

Eastern Christians and Yazides who were all over the media, claiming to be persecuted in the Muslim world. This was just ridiculous, and I wanted to scream in their faces to stop being so dramatic. They were lying, and the proof was in the history.

These communities thrived under Muslim rule. They were able to worship, work, and get educated. It was the Muslims here in the West who were being discriminated against. They did not allow us to broadcast our call to prayers. The niqab was being banned in many European countries. The Western crusading armies were invading our Muslim lands and humiliating our people. I was so frustrated with these Christians from the Middle East. They were corrupting the preimage of our religion. They were ungrateful after all that the Muslims did for them. They allowed them to live in their lands peacefully, and this is how they repay them.

I started a campaign on social media to discredit these liars out there. When Jalal found about my new mission of promoting our religion online, he was incredibly happy and encouraged to continue. I started a Facebook page and named it "Islam a religion of tolerance." On my Facebook account, I posted different historical facts and articles from various sources that undermined the claims of many of these Middle Eastern Christians that they were being discriminated against. I was not going to stand by and let these people get away with their lies.

My Facebook account became a great success. There were so many people like me who felt that we were not treated justly. I felt that someone needed to stand up to these bullies. I was not going to be silenced on this issue that was near and dear to my heart. My family was being attacked, and I intended to defend it with all my being. Jalal seemed proud of me. He asked me if I could reach out to many other young girls like myself, who were disillusioned by this corrupt Western world. He wanted me to try and get as many people as possible to convert to Islam.

I took the mantle of this cultural fight to its utmost. I wanted the whole world to know what my religion was about. I did not want these ungrateful Christian minorities to corrupt the pure image of my religion. We let them live and thrive in our Islamic world for so long. These ungrateful infidels needed to be shown for the liars that they were. My Facebook page became an instant hit. I had so many different people reaching out to me. Many young American girls found a haven with my ideas and beliefs. I became known as Aisha the spear against all infidels. It became a badge of honor for me. I was able to convert many wayward souls to my cause. Many of them went on to marry devoted Muslim men like my Jalal.

On the flip side, I attracted many haters to my Facebook account. Many of them used foul language to attack my beliefs and mission. This did not faze me one little bit. I honestly believed my mission in life was to save as many lost souls as possible. I felt under attack from these ungrateful pigs. One such debate on my Facebook page went as follows:

> "Aisha the spear against all infidels, you are nothing but a disillusioned idiot. Please read and research the history of the Middle East before giving us the wisdom of your opinions."
>
> "Whoever you are, you have no right to insult me. I know more about the Middle East than you do. The great caliphates of the past gave people of different faith and especially people of the book, meaning Jews and Christians many rights. They were able to live under the rule and thrive."
>
> "You idiot Aisha, do you really believe that? Who do you think the land the Muslims conquered belonged to before them?"
>
> "Mister, the Muslim armies did not conquer any lands from anyone they brought the true faith to unbelievers and created great empires."
>
> "Unbelievers you say. My God you are a total ignorant idiot. These lands were inhabited by people who believed in God and his son Jesus Christ. These people were Christians. Can you believe it, you idiot? Your so-called Muslim con-

quests or Futuhat-al-Islamiyya as they are called in Arabic were no better than any other conquering armies set on raping and oppressing other nations. Please do not give me all this spiel on them bringing enlightenment to the world."

"Our Prophet Mohammad peace be on to him, was a great man. He brings the word of God to many people thirsting for the truth. He gave women equal rights with man. He freed the slaves, gave grieving widows sanctuary, and lifted whole nation. The Quran is the word of God given to our Prophet. How can you argue with that you infidel?"

"As far as I am concerned your so-called Prophet was nothing, but a warlord set on conquering lands and spreading his own word not God's. He raped and killed so many people during his conquest. How can such a man be called a Prophet?" Can you answer me this quite simple question? Another point I need to point out that your kind of Islam discriminates and targets other Muslims. Look at how you kill and hurt the Shia and other Muslim sects. What about the Sunni Muslim who do not agree with you? You are prosecuted all those who oppose you. How many Muslims have you guys killed and tortured because they do not adhere to your view of Islam?"

I was aghast that such hate could be directed toward my beloved prophet, peace be unto him. I could not bear such accusations. This filthy person was targeting something so precious.

"You infidel," I wrote back. "No wonder the Islamic world is targeting you. How dare you spew such filth about our Prophet and religion? You should be killed. No one has the right to insult our Prophet without paying the consequences. Your blood should be spilled to appease our faith. You shall burn in hell you infidel. You who worship a person instead of God. You who follow a corrupt book. God sent our dearly beloved Prophet to enlighten you, yet you rejected him. May God's curse be on you and your family? May your wife and children never see a good day in their lives?"

I cursed him and blocked him from the use of my Facebook page. I did not want to hear anything about the so-called abuse my religion has inflicted on the Christians or people of different religions. I knew deep down in my heart that all this was nothing but false information. My husband was the most loving of people. He loved and supported me. He even supported his widowed mother and sister without raising an eyebrow. He took me into his family and showed me the true religion. He protected me against the world. Why would I listen to such filth from a bitter and delusional man?

After this incident I became more steeped into my faith. I turned to Jalal more and more for moral support. He encouraged me in becoming fanatical.

Traveling to Mosul and Meeting the Family

Finally, the day came for us to leave the US and visit Mosul, Jalal's hometown. I was so excited that I would finally get to see his beautiful homeland. I knew that the political situation was not the best there, but Jalal assured me not to worry for things were going to improve drastically. He made it clear that the oppressive Shia government and its forces would soon be kicked out of his beloved city and that the true heirs to Islam would once again take their rightful place.

We boarded the plane out of New York, stopped in Istanbul, and then from there we headed to Mosul. It was a long journey, and I felt constrained and uncomfortable in my Muslim garb. My daughter Amira was fussy and did not take to flying. She cried the whole two parts of the trip. She barely slept. Jalal, his mother, and sister were terribly upset with me. They kept telling me to keep the brat quiet. I did not complain because I knew that they were nervous and excited about returning to their home country. I thought to myself that when they arrived things would change drastically.

We finally landed at Mosul International Airport at two thirty in the afternoon. After we disembarked from the plane and collected our bags, we were met by a horde of relatives at the airport. They all gravitated toward Jalal, his mother, and sister. No one came near me or offered to help me with Amira and my bags. Finally, I asked Jalal for help, but he just ignored me and asked one of his relatives his carry my bag for me. He left me all by myself to deal with Amira. On the other hand, Khadija was getting the royal treatment. Her kids were fussed over, especially the boy.

I did not expect that and had thought I would get some respect because I was Jalal's wife and mother of his only child. I went to get in the car that was waiting for us. Jalal did not get in the same car as my daughter and I. I was a bit disappointed but did not think much of it. I realized that Jalal's relatives have missed them. It was no big deal. I would get to know his relatives soon enough, and I was sure they would come to love me too.

We drove through the congested streets of Mosul. We stopped at a police checkpoint. I started to panic. Why were they stopping us? I did not know it was a routine procedure. They asked for our identification papers. I gave them my American passport and was surprised when they just waved us off, without any hassle or questions. When we drove away from the checkpoint Jalal's relatives, whom I later found out were his brothers, started to swear.

Mohammad, Jalal's elder brother, said, "These sons of a whore, these lowlife Shia unbelievers. The day will come when we will kill them all. They think they can rule us. We will kill their men and rape their women."

I was shocked by what he said. I could not believe my ears. He was blatantly talking about murder and rape. I did not dare to say anything. I feared that Jalal will be terribly angry with me if talked to his brother. He had warmed multiple times that it was forbidden for a woman to talk to a male who is not related to her. When I had asked him about this peculiar edict, Jalal told me this was the prophet's way, God's peace be upon him. We do not question God's laws; we follow them.

When I asked him why I could not talk to his brothers and cousins since they were related to me through marriage, Jalal was extremely upset. His brothers were not related to me by blood. As for his cousins, even his sister was not allowed to talk to them. The only males a female can interact with, other than her husband, were her sons, bothers, blood uncles, father, and father-in-law. Every time Jalal wanted to make a point, he quoted a verse from the Quran.

"And say to the believing women that they cast down their looks and guard their private parts and do not display their ornaments except what appears thereof, and let them wear their head-coverings over their bosoms, and not display their ornaments except to their husbands or their fathers, or the fathers of their husbands, or their sons, or the sons of their husbands, or their brothers, or their brothers' sons, or their sisters' sons" (24:31).

If a woman dared talk to her husband's brothers or cousins, they would think she was coming on to them, and she would be considered a loose woman. This would reflect badly on her husband, and to save face he would be forced to beat her, or in extreme situations she would stand in front a Sharia law and would be stoned to death.

When Jalal told me this little tidbit, I thought he was just teasing me. He was jealous of other men and wanted me all for himself.

I did not want to disappoint Jalal or put him in an awkward position. It was imperative that Jalal's family think well of me. I did not want to alienate them. I was sure that my brother-in-law Mohammad spoke out of frustration.

After the second Gulf War, the Shia militants took advantage of the American occupation of Iraq and seized power. They treated the Sunni Iraqis very badly. They took all the good jobs and cut funding from the majority Sunni area. It was unfair. Many Iraqis lost their lives defending and building Iraq, and they were being marginalized. I could not condemn Mohammad's words or sentiment. I just did not agree with the mayhem-and-rape comment.

Separate Rooms

I was pondering these thoughts when we finally arrived at our accommodations. It was a spacious flat consisting of four bedrooms, two bathrooms, a living and dining area, kitchen, and a tiny room off the kitchen. It was modestly furnished, with little frills. When we entered the apartment, instead of being shown to one of the larger bedrooms, I was shown to the small room off the kitchen. Jalal had warned me beforehand not to question him, or any member of his family. The room I was shown to was four feet by four feet, had no window, and included one small single bed.

I could not understand why I was given this room. I could barely stand in it by myself, let alone share it with Jalal and our daughter Amira.

Jalal was outside in the living room with his family. I called him to me to let him know that his family had made a mistake in allocating this small room to us. I did not want to complain to him in front of his family and embarrass him. He was not happy with my calling for him.

"Aisha, what do you want? Do you know how rude and inconsiderate you are being? I have not seen my family in an awfully long time, and here you are trying to have all my attention. Aisha, you need to understand how much I missed my family and want to spend time with them. You need to learn to share me with others."

"I am really sorry, Jalal my love, I did not want to disturb or offend you. But I need to know why they put us in this tiny room? The three of us cannot fit in this room. Someone must have made a mistake."

Jalal looked at me as if I had lost my mind.

"What is wrong with this room? Be grateful for it. You and Amira will be extremely comfortable here. You do not need a bigger room."

"What do you mean Amira and me? Are you not going to share your room with us?"

"Sweetheart, you and Amira are going to occupy this room, I have been allocated another room in the house."

"What? Jalal, are you kidding me? This must be a joke. Where will my husband sleep, except in the same room as his wife?"

Jalal was taken aback by my outburst; he was used to me acquiescing to his every demand. He never thought I would question him like this, especially not in his family's home. I could see he was becoming angry at me but trying to control his temper. I started to panic and was afraid I had crossed a red line. It was eerie how afraid I was of him at that moment. I did not know what do or say. Finally, Jalal got himself under control and calmed down. With a controlled voice, he addressed me: "Aisha, my dearest wife, I mean you no disrespect, but there are things you are ignorant about. Everything will become clearer to you as time passes by. Please, my love, I am asking you not question this. Go with the flow, and life would be much easier for you and the child."

I looked at the man I loved with all my heart. Was he asking too much of me to trust things? I knew that Jalal was an important person, and I could not monopolize all his time. I knew he loved me. He married me and gave me a beautiful daughter. He respected and loved me. Out of all the women in the world, he had chosen me to marry. He shared his faith and family with me. He showed me what it was to be a good Muslim. He protected me from the outside world. Why was I questioning him? He was a good and decent man. I was lucky Aisha. I loved this man, and I was going to trust him no matter what.

Jalal would never do anything to harm and degrade me. I was his princess, his one-and-only love. How I came to regret those sentiments. Events were going to unfold that would teach me how so naive and trusting I had been. How much degradation and self-abasement were it going to take me to wake up to the reality of my situation? My stupidity and stubbornness were going to cost me a lot. This I will explain later as my life story unfolds.

Khadija Shows Her True Colors

Jalal turned around and left me with a fretful Amira, to unpack our bags and calm my daughter down. Amira was screaming and crying, refusing to calm down. She was tired and hungry. I breastfed her and was trying my best to calm her down, when Khadija burst into my room, seemingly angry and upset.

"Keep that brat quit, or else. We do not need to hear all this ruckus." She was mad, and I feared her. I felt she was going to harm my daughter.

"Khadija," I cried, "what is wrong with you? She is just a baby. She's tired, hungry, and scared. Just calm down."

"I do not care. I want her to shut up and you to stay out of my sight. You need to learn your place, you whore."

I lost my temper at this point; I had enough of Khadija and her abuse. I looked her in the eye and screamed: "You are nothing but a bitter woman! Who do you think you are? I am sick and tired of your abuse. If nothing else, I am your brother's wife and mother of his child. Jalal will hear about this. I am entitled to some respect."

"Respect, brother's wife!" she screamed. "You idiot, you have much to learn. It is about time you learned the truth about your situation. You are nothing but a fancy to Jalal. A floozy he wanted to bed, but he was forced to marry her because he is a decent and devout Muslim. He could not bed you without marriage. Do you think he loves you? I am his true love. My children are his true children. My son is his heir. Whose room do you think he will chair? You are nothing to him and his family. Your will be cast aside soon. Do not give yourself any airs. I hate you and will see you cast to the dogs."

"Khadija, that is enough!" Jalal said from the room's doorway. "Please leave and go to your room. You have overstepped your bounds, and I will deal with you later."

Khadija started sobbing and ran from the room. I have never felt so terrified in my life. I threw myself at Jalal, wanting to be consoled. I had never felt so frightened in my life. Here I was in a strange country and was verbally attacked the first day I arrived.

Sobbing, I turned to Jalal. "What is going on here? I feel I am in the twilight zone. These innuendoes and mysteries are driving me crazy. Please, I beg you, my love. What is your sister talking about? I need to know. You keep brushing my questions and concerns aside without any thought to my well-being."

Jalal looked at me with a hurt expression. He looked as if he was thinking hard about what I said. Was he going to finally tell me the truth about what was happening to Khadija?

"Aisha, listen to me. We cannot discuss this now. Khadija's problems are private. I cannot divulge her secrets. It is up to her to tell you if she wanted you to know. You as an American would understand this more than anyone else. Please trust me. Do not lose your faith in me. Are you doubting your faith and love for me? Think carefully before making such demands of me again."

I was taken aback by Jalal's statement and hurt expression. How could he doubt my love and faith in him? I gave up my world for him. He was the world for me. He was all I had. I loved him with all my being. I hated my self-doubt. What was I doing?

The Situation Is Getting Worse

After ten days of staying in Mosul, I felt it was time for us to return to the States. It was such a mistake agreeing to visit Mosul. I was homesick and knew that things in Mosul were not as rosy as Jalal and his family drew for me. I was accessing my feelings and belief system. The situation I was in was not particularly good. It did not bode well for me or my family the way I was treated. I felt like a pariah in Jalal's home. For ten days I barely saw Jalal. I was not allowed to leave his house without an escort. I felt like a prisoner.

Khadija was acting very strange. She kept gaining weight and was extremely abusive toward me. She would burst into tears one moment, and then hurl insults at me the next. I did not know what to do and felt powerless to help her. In a way I felt sorry for her. I thought she missed her deceased husband. She must be feeling lonely and sad. I knew how difficult it would be to lose someone you loved. Jalal was my world, and I could not imagine my life without him.

I sat around the house in Mosul with Jalal's female relatives, listening to them gossip and bitch and moan about the horrible situation in Mosul. They complained about how they were treated by the central government in Baghdad. They talked about how the Shia-dominated government was treating them. It was shocking how much resentment they harbored toward the Iraqi armed forces. They saw them as the enemy as the oppressors.

In a way I could sympathize with their plight. People were unlawfully detained, homes broken into, young men rounded up, and executed on the pretext of belonging to the Islamic State. It was not a safe city, and its citizens felt targeted by the Iraqi armed forces.

People wanted peace and stability and perceived the members of the Islamic State as their saviors. They envisioned a state where social justice would prevail, and the old glories of Islam would be theirs once again.

In addition, Prime Minister Nori al-Malki (a Shia politician) was extremely partisan in his actions during his term in office. He built a Shia-dominated sectarian government and refused to accommodate Sunnis. Police killed peaceful Sunni protesters and used anti-terrorism laws to mass-arrest Sunni civilians.

He refused to admit that the Shia militants were a security threat. He was adamant that the Sunni militants be disarmed before any of the Shia militants. When the American army disarmed the Sunni militants, the Shia militia came into the unarmed Sunni neighborhoods and harassed and killed many Sunnis, forcing many of them to flee for their lives. As a result, Baghdad's Sunni population went from 45 percent to 25 percent by 2007.

Al-Maliki opposed the integration of the "Awakening Councils"—armed Sunnis willing to fight extremists—into the armed forces. He feared they might create problems for his Shiite-dominated government after the defeat of al-Qaeda. Instead of hiring one hundred thousand Sunni Awakening Council fighters in Mosul and Fallujah, he only hired seventeen thousand of them, leaving eighty-three thousand fighters without stipends or pensions. These fighters eventually turned against the government and joined ISIS.

Maliki showed preferential treatment toward Shia towns and cities. He refused to help develop the country's economy and depended heavily on income coming from oil. He kept the Iraqi army weak, fearing a coup against him. He viciously put down any dissent against him and behaved like a dictator. He also disregarded the election of the Sunni representatives. In late 2011, Vice President Tariq al-Hashimi was arrested on the grounds of terrorism without due process. All these actions helped to pave the way for ISIS's tentacles spreading in Sunni-dominated areas.

All this was blamed on the occupying American forces. They had toppled the legitimate Iraqi President Saddam Hussein and put in its stead a corrupt pro-Iranian Shia government that was trying to suppress the Iraqi Sunnis. Everyone knows that Shia are a heretical group that had always tried to suppress the Sunni. It was intolerable. No wonder these people were upset and wanted nothing to do with the central government.

ISIS Takes Over

A date when my life changed irrevocably was June 10, 2014, when the Islamic State of Iraq and the Levant (ISIL) insurgents, initially led by Abu Abdulrahman al-Bilawi, defeated the Iraqi Army led by Lieutenant General Mahdi Al-Gharrawi. At first, I thought, finally, our aim to overthrow the despot government and establish God's rule on earth was a reality. God had guided our forces against the oppressors. Everyone was elated. Everything was going to be great. We were finally going to go home. Our mission here was finished. I was homesick and wanted to return to the States.

Jalal was very busy during this time. He did not come home for days, and I was told specifically to stay indoors since it was not safe yet to walk the streets of Mosul. There were still progovernment forces that were wreaking havoc on the local population. Jalal needed to meet with the newly appointed liberators of Mosul. Since he had played such a major role in the liberation of Mosul, he was going to be awarded a major role in the new order. I missed him a lot but understood that he needed to be part of this great time.

I had to spend time with Jalal's female relatives. Let's just say I felt that I was not really accepted as part of their group. Khadija and Jamila (Jalal's other sister) were extremely close. Each one of them had a large room in the house. I kept wondering where Jamila's husband was. They had told me she could not have children and that was why her husband left her. I felt extremely sorry for her, even though she ignored me most of the time.

Khadija, on the other hand, kept gaining weight. She was become very bitter and did not stop snapping at me. She did not

75

even try to hide her hatred toward me. I did not want to rock the boat with Jalal. I felt he had enough on his plate as it is. He did not have the time to deal with his sister now. I thought things would get better once we returned to the States. I felt that when we returned, I would ask Jalal if we could have our own home. I knew we could afford it. I could get a job and finish my degree. I was living in my own world. I did not want to see what was before my eyes.

According to Jalal and his family, the situation on the ground was getting better. The liberating forces were undoing years of corruption and helping fix the mess left by the pro-Shia government. It was imperative for them to reestablish the just and divine Sharia law. ISIS fighters and volunteers were working hard to make Mosul a better place to live. They set tariffs for waste disposal and banned litter. Anyone caught throwing away waste would incur a fine of twenty-five thousand dinars (twenty-two dollars) or imprisoned if they refused to pay the fine. This was great news for me. Finally, they were going to clean the city up. What a great thing to happen.

Along the River Euphrates, ISIS banned fishing during spawning season and the use of dynamite for fishing. They also banned the use of electric-current fishing. Electric-current fishing is when two electrodes deliver a current into the water. This leads to the extermination of many water creatures and the congenital disfigurement for small fish and other river creatures. I was really impressed by this ban. These fighters were taking care of the environment. I was so proud of my adopted faith. This faith was protecting the environment.

What a feat these soldiers of God have accomplished. In the West, we have destroyed our environment. We hunt, kill, and overfish our oceans. We have polluted our air, land, and waterways. We like to preach to other developed nations while we are destroying our planet with our greed and selfishness. We are unable to compromise on a law that will protect our environment. If this was not proof of the rightness of the Islamic State, then I do not know what more I can say.

Things were really improving. The population of Mosul saw the Islamic forces as liberators from the oppressive central government situated in Baghdad. People were optimistic and happy. Finally, in power was a group that would protect their interests. When ISIS took control, they treated people decently, clearing all the checkpoints scattered around Mosul by the army and clearing the roads. The residents of Mosul were ecstatic that the Shia Army was no more, and all detainees and bribes. Residents were sick and tired of bribing officials to get things down.

Sister or Wife?

A couple of weeks after the liberation of Mosul by ISIS, things started to get much clearer. My world took such a drastic turn for the worse. My elation at the liberation of Mosul became an afterthought. I could not believe what a naive and deluded person I had become. I had always prided myself on being a shrewd judge of character. All the signs were right before my eyes, but I was so blinded by my arrogance that I did not see them. I was a pathetic individual who had no one to blame but herself. My family and friends had warned me of the dire consequences of my actions, but I scoffed at them and belittled their concern.

Jalal had just arrived home from a week of absence. I was elated to see him. I ran to him and threw my arms around him.

"Jalal, you are home, my love," I said. "I was so worried about you. Thank God for your safety."

I was so happy to see him. I was so worried about him. I felt homesick and wanted him to take me back home. I knew I should not have put much pressure on him. He had a lot on his plate, but I could not help myself.

Instead of hugging me back, Jalal pushed me aside. He looked at me with concern. It was the first time I had seen Jalal look at me in this manner. It was eerie. He either looked at me with lust or anger, but never with concern. Something was up, but for the life of me I could not figure out what it was.

"Tina, we need to talk. You need to know the truth about our lives."

The tone of his voice made me apprehensive. A felt a chill enter my body. I was getting frightened. It must really be a serious topic he wanted to broach to me. I knew that I had not broken any of his rules and edicts. I was modest, did not argue with any of his family, prayed five times a day, took care of my daughter and Khadija's children, cooked, and cleaned. What was so important that he was taking this tone with me? Did he want to send me and Amira, our daughter, back to the States without him? All these thoughts kept swirling in my mind. I was going crazy overthinking this. I needed to calm down and listen to Jalal. I needed to trust him.

Taking a deep breath, I tried calming myself down.

"Jalal, my love, there is nothing you can tell me that would shock me. I left my world to be with you. I cut ties with my family and friends to be faithful to you and our Muslim faith. I know you love me. You have been under tremendous pressure, and I understand I need to stand by your side in good and bad times."

Jalal tried to interrupt my speech, but I continued in the same vein, trying to reassure him of my loyalty and love.

"Now that Mosul is liberated, we can return home. My dearest, I am homesick. I know how much you sacrificed to liberate your city. That is why I love you so much. You are a man of principle. We need to get back to the States to spread our faith."

"Aisha," Jalal interrupted my impassioned speech. "Listen to me. What you are about to hear does not go against my faith. You called me a man of principles, and it is true I am. I follow my faith to the letter. The prophet himself, God's peace upon him, urged us to follow his example. He was a perfect man, and we all strive to emulate his example. We are called on to marry and multiply."

What Jalal was saying was true. That was why he married me. We have a daughter, and God willing we would have more children.

"Yes, I know, my love. You married me, we have a daughter whom we love a lot, and God willing I would give more children very soon. Sons and daughters that would carry on your legacy. Hopefully, a son who would carry the banner of our faith to the world. Inshallah, soon we would conquer the world with our faith."

Jalal looked at me with amazement, as if I had two heads. He started laughing out loud. "Aisha, my dear, Inshallah we have dozens of children. You have been a good and faithful wife. I have been so proud of you. You have made me proud. You, born an infidel, converted to the true religion and lived as a faithful Muslim better than other people who were born Muslims. I cannot tell you how much this means to me. I might have married you because I desired you, but I thank Allah every day for having you in my life."

I felt as if I had been given the world. I never dreamed that Jalal would say these words to me. My eyes were tearing. I could not help myself; I just threw myself at Jalal, hugging and kissing him.

Jalal patted my head, tilted my head, and looked at me with such love that I felt precious. I was his little princess. I knew he was under a lot of pressure and knew he could relax and show me how much he loved and cared for me.

Suddenly, Khadija entered the room, screaming: "Jalal, tell this woman the truth! I am tired of hiding the truth from her. Don't you think I have suffered enough? Our Prophet God blessing unto him, decreed that a man can have up to four wives. It is our way and our religion. Stop trying to shield her from the truth. She is a Muslim woman now and needs to accept reality. To survive and preserve our faith, we had to put up with this lie. Just tell her. She needs to know her place in the larger scheme of things."

I looked between the two. What was Khadija talking about? As always, she was angry about something or someone. What have I done now? Could she not give me a break? I was sick and tired of her insults and snide remarks. I just had enough. I needed to know what was going on. I had been living in ignorance for a long time.

"Jalal," Khadija continued her tirade, "I have had enough of this farce. What you are doing is haram. I am going to tell my family if you do not tell her. You know how powerful they are. They can make your life a living hell."

I knew that something was serious here. At the same time, I was really confused by her statement. What did she mean by her family? Jalal was her brother. He was her family. Why was she threatening her own flesh and blood? The person who took care of her and her family. He sacrificed so much for them, and here she was threatening him. Was she deranged?

Jalal looked angry. He backhanded Khadija, and she fell to the floor. I ran to help her, but she slapped my hands away and screamed at me: "Don't touch me, you bitch!"

Jalal looked at Khadija and said in a threatening voice, "Woman, do not ever threaten me again. I do not think this family will take kindly to your behavior. You are a mere woman. Know your place. As a devoted woman, you know what the holy Quran says."

In Surah 4:34, Allah revealed to the prophet, "Men are in charge of women, because Allah hath made the one of them to excel the other."

Surah 4:34 says, "So good women are the obedient, guarding in secret that which Allah hath guarded. As for those from whom ye fear rebellion, admonish them and banish them to beds apart, and scourge them."

After quoting these two verses from the Quran, Jalal continued in the same voice: "Your family might have influence, but I do too. I could divorce you, and no one would question me. I will take your children away from you, and you will never see them again. You have been a great and loyal wife to me, but do not ever try to threaten me again. I have given you too much say and influence. I wanted to respect and honor you. In return I got a harpy who does not know her place."

Taking a deep breath, he continued: "Do you hear me, woman? I can beat you for your insolence and disrespect. Stop your screaming and screeching, get off the floor, and get to your room. I will not be so lenient with you next time."

Khadija started crying and wailing, asking Jalal for forgiveness. She grabbed his hand and started kissing it. It was like watching a scene out of a movie. I have never seen Khadija so humble. In a way a felt vindicated, but still completely baffled by the exchange between the two. Why did he threaten to divorce her, his own sister? I have never heard Jalal talk to Khadija in this manner. Finally, she got off the floor. She took Jalal's hand, kissed it, and went to her room.

I suddenly felt terrified of the situation. The blinds were suddenly being lifted from my eyes. This was not right.

Jalal finally looked at me.

"I think you guessed the truth, Aisha."

I shook my head in denial. I could not believe the truth staring me in the face.

"I need to hear the truth directly from your own lips. You have manipulated and lied to me all this time. Tell me the truth. Tell me the truth!" I screamed. "Is it true? Khadija is your wife? How can this be true? I do not understand any of it."

Jalal looked me straight in the eyes, and without hesitation, said, "Yes, Khadija is my wife. Her children are mine, and she is pregnant with my fourth child. She is dear to me, and I respect and love her."

I fell to the ground, sobbing. I could not believe all this. I wanted to deny his words. Was I so blinded that I did not see the little hints that were there for a blind person to see? What was I going to do? I wanted to go home, back to my family, to the people who love and really care for me. I had no one here to depend on. I was just a means to an end for Jalal and his family.

"How can you do this to me? Is our marriage even legal? Polygamy is illegal in the USA. Why did you pretend to marry me and get me with child if you already had a wife and children? Khadija is pregnant with your fourth child. Oh my god, you were sleeping with her at the same time you were sleeping with me. Is that why you isolated me from your family, so that no one would tell me the truth? I would never have married you if I had known the truth. You took the choice away from me. You forced me in a situation because of my ignorance. I do not blame Khadija for hating me. I took her husband away from her. You cheated with me on her and vice versa. How could you?"

"Listen, Aisha. Believe me, our marriage is legal in here and in the USA. I divorced Khadija in the American courts to marry you, but I did not divorce her in the Sharia law. I do not recognize the American courts because it is contrary to the Sharia. I had to go through all this to get you to marry me. I needed an American wife, and I liked your looks."

"Are you telling me that you only lusted after me? I am no more than a body to you? You do not cherish me. You do not respect me. Oh my god. I gave up my whole life for you. I alienated my friends and family to be with you. I left my country and everything dear to me to be with you. What have you done? You destroyed me and my faith in you."

"Aisha you knew Islam permits more than one wife. Allah and the prophet, peace be upon, him decreed it."

Quran (4:3): "Marry of the women, who seem good to you, two or three or four; and if ye fear that ye cannot do justice (to so many) then one (only) or (the captives) that your right hands possess."

Jalal grabbed my arm, trying to calm me down. His actions sent me over the edge.

I started hitting him and screaming obscenities. How could the man I put above all else do this to me? This man I loved with all my heart and soul. He already had a wife. This man who I thought was perfect. Heart-wrenching sobs were heard, and I did not know until later that the sounds were coming from me.

All I wanted was to grab my daughter and escape Jalal's presence and this godforsaken country.

"Why are you acting like a crazy woman? In Islam we do not recognize any law except what God gave us though his Prophet Mohammad, God's peace upon him. The Sharia and Quran are ultimate sources of law and how to live our lives."

He stopped for a second and then continued in a patronizing voice, "Believe me, we are legally married. You and Amira belong to me. Do you understand this? While we are at it, there is another truth you need to know about. The woman Ume Afran, whom you thought was a widow, is Khadija's cousin and my second wife. I married her because she was a childless war widow who needed a home. You see, my compassion has no end. She would have starved on the streets if I had not married her. Unlike you, she is grateful to the honor bestowed upon her. She respects me and my children. She adores Khadija and does all she wants. You need to learn from her."

"What the hell, are you telling me? That you have a third wife? That the lady who takes care of Khadija and your kids is your wife?

Oh my god. You are disgusting person. She is grateful? I cannot believe what I am hearing. Are you for real? You could have helped her without marrying her and treating her like a slave to you wife and your kids. Instead, you married her to have a servant and another bedmate. You are nothing but a brute."

Taking a deep breath, I let all my frustration out. This was all unbelievable. I could not tolerate looking at him, let alone fathom the idea that this man was my husband.

"I do not belong to you, and my daughter is mine. I am a free-thinking woman. I am no one's property. Do you hear me? I am no one's property. Do not give me any spiel about how it is in the Quran or Hadith. I am sick and tired of you treating me as an idiot. I am leaving here and going back home. I am an American citizen, and I have rights. I will not tolerate you or your disgusting behavior. Stay away from me and my child. Do you hear me, you animal?"

Jalal slapped me so hard across the face that I fell to the floor. He stepped over me and grabbed me by my hair, causing me severe pain

"Listen to me very carefully, Aisha," he said very calmly.

In my anger I did not heed him. I screamed at him in rage. "My name is Tina, not Aisha! Do you hear me? Tina is my name. Tina, Tina, Tina!" I kept screaming this in his face. I could not stop. I was angry and frustrated and had lost my temper. I could hear my daughter crying and screaming for me from my little closet room, but I was blind and deaf to everything going on except my anger and disgust at Jalal. Continuing my tirade, I screamed at him, "When you gave me the name Aisha, I thought I was someone special to you! But obviously I am nothing to you but a sexual tool and a baby incubator. I will not listen to you anymore. I have had about more than I can take from you and your abusive family. I have never been treated with such contempt and hatred in my life. Who do you think you are to treat me in such a manner? A lying bigamist. A person with no honor and principles. You even gave me a broom closet and set you precious Khadija in the largest bedroom. You made me take care of your ill-mannered children. I cannot believe this."

I felt as if I was in a nightmare, waiting to wake up and find myself back home in the States. This was so surreal.

Tears were stinging my eyes. I could not stop all that was coming out of my mouth. I was not going to pretend anymore that everything was fine. I had been lying to myself. I had based my whole identity on a lie. A lie that I wholeheartedly believed in. A lie that I defended against anyone who dared criticize it. I trusted a man who had abused me and lied to me. This was madness. What have I done to myself?

As all these thoughts entered my mind, Jalal was pulling at my hair. I felt as if my hair was going to be torn from its roots. I felt as if I was living a nightmare with no way out. I wanted to wake up but could not. I ignored the severe pain. I could not be quiet anymore. I had reached my boiling point. What was the point anymore? What I thought I had, it had shattered in front of my eyes. I wanted to denigrate Jalal and his family. He had used and abused me for the last time. I was leaving him as soon as I could. Let him say and do what he wanted. I was not his property. I was no one's property. I was taught in Islam that women had rights, and I was about to assert my rights. Little did I know that this was just the tip of the iceberg. I was his to do as he wanted. I was literally his prisoner.

Qs 16:97 says the same thing, with a slightly different emphasis: "Whoever does good whether male or female and he is a believer, We will most certainly make him live a happy life, and We will most certainly give them their reward for the best of what they did."

I had studied the Quran and knew the verse I needed to quote: "You see, Jalal, in Islam God gave me rights. I am leaving you. Do you hear me? I am leaving you. Take your hands off me and never touch me again. I am going to be sick. How could you treat me this way? What have I ever done to you? I do not deserve your treatment. You have deceived me for the last time. Your touch disgusts me. I hate you. If I can kill you where you stand, I would. I cannot take any more of this."

In a very controlled voice, Jalal said, "I would not repeat myself again, Aisha. You seized to be Tina the day you converted to Islam. If you think you have rights under the Islamic State, then think again.

The Prophet Mohammad, peace be upon him, made women inferior to men. They are nothing but his chattels. Do you want me to quote from the Quran to prove my point?

Quran (2:223): "Your wives are as a tilth unto you; so approach your tilth when or how ye will…" A man has dominion over his wives' bodies as he does his land.

Al-Tirmidhi 3272: "When Allah's Messenger was asked which woman was best he replied, 'The one who pleases (her husband) when he looks at her, obeys him when he gives a command, and does not go against his wishes regarding her person or property by doing anything of which he disapproves'."

"Well, Jalal do you really want to quote from the Quran and Islamic scholars, what about the verse [3:195] Their Lord responded to them: 'I never fail to reward any worker among you for any work you do, be you male or female—you are equal to one another. Thus, those who immigrate, and get evicted from their homes, and are persecuted because of Me, and fight and get killed, I will surely remit their sins and admit them into gardens with flowing streams.'" Such is the reward from God. God possesses the ultimate reward.

"Do not use this logic with me. The hell with you, Jalal. Again, I repeat myself. My name is Tina. I am an American born and raised. I have rights. You cannot take them away from me." My emotions were arriving at a boiling point. Unfortunately, I did not heed his warning. I was blind to my rage and did not heed my speech. I was not thinking clearly. That was my biggest mistake.

Laughing, Jalal shoved me to the ground and proceeded to beat me up. Blows came at me like crazy. He was a man possessed. He kicked and punched me hard. I felt as if every bone in my body was going to break.

While he was beating me, he screamed at me: "I will do with you as I wish! Hear me well, Aisha. I will bed you when I want. You are mine. Do you hear me? You belong to me and only me for the time being. Remember that. I will give you to my commander when I have had my fill of you. Do not presume to tell me what to do. You will follow my rules. As far as you are concerned, you are nothing but my possession. I own you and my daughter. Do you hear? My daughter, not yours. She belongs to me and only me. Do not even think that you will have any say in her upbringing. I have already contracted a marriage contract between her and our prince. Once she is twelve years old, I will marry her off. By that time, God willing, you would give more children. You will not deny anything I ask for." He kept hitting me as he told me all that.

Finally, he let me up. He grabbed me by the ankle and dragged me across the room to my room. He then slammed the door close and left. By that time I had lost consciousness.

Samira, Jalal's Aunt

I came to consciousness to Jalal's aunt Samira, who was sitting next to me and comforting Amira. She was also wiping at my wounds in a soothing manner. I looked at her with fear. I did not know whom to trust, or who to turn to. She was Jalal's paternal aunt, and I feared her attitude toward me and my daughter. I tried to get up and snatch my daughter from her hands. I did not know if she was here to gloat. She gently urged me back to bed, and for the first time since I came to this forsaken country someone was showing me some kindness. It was exceedingly difficult for me to trust her.

"My dear, please do not get up. I know you have every reason to hate and despise my family, but you have a lot to learn about us. I might seem tough on the outside, but this was all an act. Our family is not as uniform in our beliefs."

Stammering and in great pain, I scoffed at her words. "You all hate me. I am the American infidel who married the golden boy."

"Habibati [meaning my love, an endearment in Arabic], believe me, we do not hate you. We did not trust you. We thought you were one of them. These people who want to oppress and destroy our way of life. They have distorted our religion and beliefs. I am a proud and faithful Muslim. But I do not follow Jalal's extreme view of my beloved religion. We are tolerant and love others. We lived alongside people of different faiths. We respected their beliefs, and they respected ours. Jalal is not a true Muslim. He is a follower of a distorted version of Islam. His wife, Khadija, and her family brainwashed him. Growing up, Jalal was a sweet and tolerant boy. He loved life and respected others. His father, my brother, God rest his soul, was a decent and good man."

I was shocked by what she was revealing. Could I believe what she was saying? I did not know what to say.

She continued in a gentle and compassionate voice, "My dear, believe me when I tell you, Jalal and his family were never like this. They were a beautiful family. My father was loved by all. He prayed and fasted but was tolerant of people's different views. He used to say that there was no compulsory in religion."

Say, "O disbelievers, I do not worship what you worship. Nor are you worshippers of what I worship. Nor will I be a worshipper of what you worship. Nor will you be worshippers of what I worship. For you is your religion and for me is my religion" Quran 109*:1–6.

Continuing in her speech: "We have been brought up to be tolerant and accepting of others. We are not radical. My father did not force me or any of my sisters to wear the veil. He said it was our choice. This is real Islam. My dear, you have been blinded by a zealot. I love my nephew, but I do not agree with him on how he is conducting is life.

"Jalal was a Baathist [the party that ruled Iraq under Saddam Hessian]. He did not adhere to the strict teachings of Wahhabi Islam. He was popular and was loved by all. He had friends from all walks of life and religions. When he was in his early twenties, he met Khadija's brother, Mohammad, who was extremely religious. He brainwashed Jalal. Jalal idolized him and felt he was incredibly wise. He wanted to be like him. No arguments from our family could sway Jalal. He felt we were betraying our faith. I thank God every day that all my children have left Iraq. They avoided any form of brainwashing. Do not misunderstand me. They are devoted Muslims but do not approve of Jalal's version of Islam. My late brother would not have approved of his actions. As for my sister-in-law, his mother, she is weak and easily manipulated. Take heart, my love, things will improve.

"He introduced him to Khadija, and they got married. At first, we were skeptical that this marriage would work. Khadija was deeply religious and strict. She made my family's life hell. Eventually my sister-in-law had no choice but to acquiescence to her. She had no choice. She did not want to lose her son. As time went by, my mother also became brainwashed.

"When Jalal met you, we were ecstatic. He fell hard for you. We felt that Khadija's influence on him might wane. Unfortunately, that was not the case. He felt so guilty about talking a third wife that he had to overcompensate for falling in love with you."

Looking at me with pity and concern, Samira continued with her story. I was slowly fading away from the pain and hurt that I had just experienced. I did not want to listen to Samira, but I had no choice.

"In the case of his second wife Um Afran [her actual name is Suha], there was no comparison. She was a childless widow who Khadija wanted to add to her household. She felt she could use her as an obedient servant. Suha was not a threat to her. She was her cousin. She never considered her as an equal. She is very loyal to Khadija. Jalal never felt any physical attraction to her. He felt sorry for her and wanted to give her a home. She was Khadija's cousin, and that was the only way he could help her.

"Suha is very loyal to Khadija and her family. She will do anything for them. She is an extremely dangerous person. I do not think she is stable."

Looking disturbed and upset, Samira could not hide her dismay with the situation.

"I think there is something wrong with the whole family. They are dangerous, and it behooves anyone to cross them.

"I have seen and heard things about them that will turn your hair white. They have destroyed life."

Samira took a deep breath and released it. I felt her anguish and concern over the situation. She exhaled and continued in her explanation.

"During that time, many of our people, especially young Sunni men, felt alienated from the government. They felt harassed, mistreated, and scared. They felt they had no future. No one represented them or addressed their concerns. ISIS played on their fears and concerns. They positioned themselves as the voice to the voiceless, the saviors of the Sunni population. Many young Sunni men saw them as their salvation. Finally, there was someone who understood their concerns. Someone who would stand up for their rights.

"Let me tell you something, my dear. The United States government did my beloved country no favors when they got rid of President Saddam Hussein. Yes, he was a tyrant, but at least he established law and order. People felt safe. People of all religions were treated equally, as long as they kept to themselves and did not get involved in politics.

"When the regime fell, we were overrun by the Shia militants. They jailed our men, tortured and killed them. All this resulted in a backlash. Unfortunately, the backlash went too far. I am heartbroken for my country and my beloved city.

"Rest now, my dear, let me take care of the little one. Remember to keep a low profile, and do not engage my nephew or his vicious wife in any argument. Please, I beg you, listen to me very carefully. I cannot help you all the time. I will do my best, but you need to heed my warning. The situation is going to get worse for a while, but God willing, I pray for change for the better. Do not despair. I beg you, just play along and try to blend in. Let Jalal believe you have accepted his edict."

Continuing with her advice, Samira went on to say that the whole family was praying for Jalal to open his eyes to the reality of these murderous thugs. In her opinion, a time would come when this nightmare would come to an end. She beseeched me never to give up hope and pray that Jalal would come to his senses.

Samira hugged my baby to her heart and left me to sleep. I was slowly losing consciousness and just wanted the oblivion of sleep.

Deteriorating Situation

The horror of my life was a never-ending saga. Why was I here in this living hell on earth? These people have established their Islamic State on the corpses of the innocent people who lived in the area. It was a bloody and vicious war, with no laws or rules guiding it. These people were animals. They had no respect for anything or anyone. They came like hordes of beasts killing and maiming everyone in their path, not caring whom they harmed in their way.

In the Name of Allah and his Prophet Mohammad, they committed so many atrocities that in the end I became numb to all that was happening around me. Human life was nothing but a commodity to be traded around. Women became possessions to be bartered for. I became a victim because of my ignorance and rigid thinking. I cannot describe to you the hell I went through. The years I lived as a willing and then unwilling captive to my ignorance and resolve not to see all that was in front of my very eyes.

The situation in Mosul deteriorated rapidly. The euphoria that prevailed in the Sunni community with the ISIL occupation of Mosul was quickly replaced by dejection and misery. ISIS implemented laws and regulations that restricted people's movements, the way they dressed, and their behavior. Certain dress codes were severely enforced for both men and women. Men were beheaded if they shaved their beards, and women were whipped if they were not covered from head to toe in black.

Children were required to attend ISIL-run schools where ISIL curriculum was taught. Students were indoctrinated with ISIL mentality. The economic situation declined drastically. Food, water, and other necessities were in short supply. Prices soared drastically. Hospitals ran out of medical supplies, and all women doctors were forced to leave their jobs. Male doctors were not allowed to examine women, and as the female doctors were prohibited from working, female patients suffered the most. The situation had become so bad.

Mobile phones were confiscated from the populace, and merely possessing a SIM card was punishable by death. No one could speak against the situation or complain. Anyone caught drinking alcohol, smoking cigarettes, or taking drugs was put to death. It was a totalitarian regime with one ideology to follow. You follow its rules, or you were put to death. No one could leave Mosul.

Comply or Get Punishment

Screaming and crying woke me from a deep sleep. My heart was beating erratically in my chest. My hands were sweating, and my head was throbbing. I got out of my mattress on the floor in the corner of the sitting room and went to check on Amira. She was sleeping peacefully.

The screaming and crying got louder and louder. I was terrified something major was going on. Usually, I avoided Khadija like the plague, but this time I really wanted to find out what was going on.

Spying her in the living room, I called out to her in a respectful voice: "Khadija, what is going on? The screaming is really scary. What is all this noise? Is something going on? Are we under attack?"

Khadija looked at me with derision and started to laugh. "Do you really want to know what is going on? Can you handle it?"

I was so desperate that I started to beg Khadija: "Please, Khadija, for the love of God, let me know what is going on. Please, I beg you, I am really scared. Just tell me what is going on."

"All right, Aisha, I will not only tell you what is going on, I will show you. Put your niqab and gloves on and follow me. Aunt Samira will keep an eye on Amira."

I hurried and donned on my niqab and gloves and followed Khadija. I was not allowed to leave the house by myself. I always needed an escort. On the other hand, Khadija could come and go as she pleased because her teenage son would accompany her. She was a member the Al-Khansaa Brigade compromised of women loyal to the Islamic State. The Al-Khansaa Brigade were members of Daish

ISIS." They patrolled the streets of Mosul, looking for women not following the Islamic State dress code and behavior.

The Al-Khansaa Brigade's job was to raise awareness of their religion among women, and to punish women who do not abide by the Islamic law. They monitor women, ensuring they adhered to ISIS rules. Jihad, I was told, was not only the domain of men, but women need to do their part as well. The brigade has its own facilities to avoid mingling men and women. They were created to terrorize women.

They approach women in public, pointing the firearms at them. They then would test their knowledge of prayer, fasting, and hijab. They would snatch and detain women if they saw them walking without an escort, or wearing their hijab incorrectly. According to Khadija, the crimes committed by women vary from breastfeeding outside to not wearing black socks or high heels.

The Al-Khamsaa Brigade would punish a woman with at least forty lashes for wearing the wrong clothes. They'd flog, imprison, and publicly punish people in iron cages. They enforced attendance of mandatory religious sessions and collect fines from violators. Most of Al-Khansaa members were married to ISIS members.

I really did not want to go out with Khadija on her sadist trip. She was six months pregnant with Jalal's son, and I knew she had a lot of sway with him. I feared what she might say to him. She took great pleasure in causing trouble for me. He had already threatened to rip my daughter from my arms and give me to his leader, who happened to be Khadija's brother. I was in quagmire that was hard to get out of.

Jalal always took Khadija's side in any argument. Her hatred and resentment had not abated in the least. She wanted to destroy me and wipe any evidence of me from existence. She knew Jalal's family did not like her, but she did not care. She had a powerful family behind her. She still respected and feared Jalal, but at the same time she knew that she held sway over Jalal. She was the perfect pious female warrior, fighting for her faith. It was scary how committed she was to her cause. I feared her. I never wanted to be on her bad side. She found any opportunity to demean and belittle me.

Thrown in Prison

I followed Khadija out of Jalal's modest house into the streets. Before leaving, I made sure that I was covered from head to toe, without anything showing. I did not want a repeat of what happened the last time I went out with Khadija.

It was an extremely hot afternoon, and Khadija was in one of her happy moods, and she asked me to accompany her to the souk, to buy food for our dinner. I took this opportunity to escape the stifling confines of the house. As we were headed to the souk, I heard screaming and shouting. Then suddenly five armed females, covered from head to toe, descended upon us hurling insults. One of them forced me to my knees and pointed a gun to my head.

"Why are you dressed like a harlot?" one of the women screamed.

"Are you trying to seduce our men?" another said.

"Your hands are showing, you are not wearing dark socks, and your veil is sheer," yet another claimed.

"You are a disgrace to your father and husband, you need to be whipped,"

The group of ladies then dragged me with them to be further interrogated. I tried to appeal to Khadija to come to my rescue, but she just left me to my fate.

I pleaded with Khadija to help me. Crying and begging for mercy.

"Please, I beg you. I did not know I needed to wear gloves and black stockings. Please, I beg you. Let me go. It is the last time I will ever leave the house without gloves and black stockings."

My stockings were dark, but it seemed not dark enough for these women. In my haste to follow Khadija, I forgot my gloves.

I begged and begged to be released. All my pleas fell on deaf ears. Khadija was laughing at me. I was terrified of what was going to happen to me.

I was taken to a detention center (jail) in the middle of the city, which used to be a girls' school before ISIS took over. They shut down the school and turned it into a detention center. There were two entrances, one for the females and the other for males. Segregation needed to be observed in all aspects of life.

I was thrown into a cell. The cell was small, dark, dank, and dirty. It smelled of urine and feces. I could barely breathe. I have heard of the horrors inflicted on female prisoners by the Al-Khansaa Brigade. They were ruthless toward anyone they considered the enemy. I also knew that Khadija had orchestrated this whole incident. She wanted to humiliate and hurt me. She was unscrupulous in her behavior toward anyone she deemed a threat. She did not care who she hurt if she got her way. Deep down inside, I knew she was mentally unbalanced.

She had been for some time regaling me with all the terrifying stories of the greatness of the enforcers of the faith. Khadija wanted me to suffer deeply. The mere images that were floating in my mind petrified me. She related a terrifying story of how women who were not dressed properly were punished by the "biter" or "clipper," a metal instrument that causes immense pain by clipping off pieces of flesh. Fatima said this instrument had teeth that cut into the flesh.

An Al-Khansaa member came to question me. She kept screaming in my face and slapping me. I was crying and asking for mercy. She laughed at me and spat in my face.

Finally, she said that I would be whipped fifty lashes in public, and my husband would administer my punishment. I was to stay in the cell until my husband came and took me to the central square where my punishment would be administered. I was so scared. I had left my baby at home with my mother-in-law and was afraid that she would not take care of her properly. Samira was not feeling well and had no choice but to leave her with my mother-in-law.

I was terrified of Jalal's reaction. I was convinced that he was going to take great pleasure in my suffering. He had warned me multiple times about being demure and decent in my dress and behavior. He would be so ashamed of me. I burst into tears and could not stop crying. Finally, I was so exhausted that I fell asleep on the floor of the dirty cell.

Jalal Came to Prison

A kick in my side woke me up. I looked up and found myself starring at Jalal. He was furious. His face contorted in outrage and pain. I was afraid for my life. He looked as if he could murder me with his bare hands. I scrambled away from him, and my back hit the cell wall.

Jalal grabbed me by the hair and started screaming at me.

"You bitch, do you know what you have done? You have humiliated me in front of my peers. You put yourself on display for the whole world to see."

I knew Jalal was possessive of me and feared other men might want me for themselves. Samira, his aunt, had explained his fear of losing me. He was obsessed with me. He could not fathom anyone not wanting me. His jealousy was not healthy. Khadija played on his feelings for me to make him jealous and to suspect me of contemplating adultery. She kept telling how other men might desire me. This was her way of seeking revenge on me. She wanted Jalal to cast me aside to be his number-one wife. She dragged to the souk without telling me I was not dressed properly. She wanted Jalal to see how I was flaunting myself in front other men. This was guaranteed to enrage him. She played her role very well. Jalal was enraged, and I was going to pay the price.

Jalal was frightened by what was about to happen. He knew I had to be publicly punished by him. He did not want to be weak in front of his peers, but at the same time he did not want to hurt me. He was put in a very delicate position. Khadija had played her hand very smartly. She knew that my dress was going to get me into trouble, and she relished the fact. She was a diabolical bitch. I did

not know how to fight her. Jalal, with all his faults, was my only protection against her.

I was really frightened. I could not endure fifty lashes. I knew I
was a coward, but I started to beg Jalal for mercy.

"Jalal," I cried out, "I beg you, please do not hurt me. I did not
know that I was dressed inappropriately. It is the first time I have
left the house. I did not know any better. Please, I beseech you, have
mercy on me. I promise to do whatever you want. I cannot bear fifty
lashes. In the name of Allah the merciful and his prophet, peace be
upon him. I ask for mercy."

I got on my knees and grabbed his hand and kissed it. I begged
him with all my heart and soul. I was terrified of the consequences
of my actions.

"I beg you, Jalal, have mercy on me. I did not know that I was
doing anything wrong. I am sorry, I am sorry, I am sorry. Please do
not let them whip me. Khadija asked me to accompany her and did
not tell me anything about my dress. She insisted that I go with her
to the souk. Please again, I beg you."

Tears were streaming from my eyes. My body was shaking from
fear. What more could I say? I was terrified of the whole situation.
I knew I could not handle this kind of abuse. Khadija had tricked
me. She wanted to embarrass Jalal for him to reject me. She knew he
loved me and wanted to hurt me as much as possible. She was one of
the most vindictive women I had encountered. Deep down inside, I
knew how much Jalal was struggling. He did not want to see me hurt
but wanted to do what he thought was right. He genuinely believed
that he was doing the right thing. He genuinely loved me, but he was
put in an exceedingly difficult situation.

Finally, Jalal let go of my hair. He turned away from me and left
the prison cell. I collapsed on the floor, sobbing. I did not know what
was going to happen to me. I knew that my transgression needed to
be addressed, but I prayed for a more merciful punishment. After
what seemed like hours to me, Jalal finally returned. He looked at
me in a most tender manner. I have never seen him look at me in
this manner. He looked as if he really cared. He gently took me in his
arms and carried me out of the prison cell. He carried me through

the prison building toward the exit, where a car was waiting outside. We got in the car with me still in his arms. The car drove us through the streets until we got to our house.

The Truth Comes Out

We got out of the car and entered our house. Khadija was waiting for us. She had a malicious smile on her face. She was waiting for me to arrive.

"Well, here is our whore," she said in a scornful manner. "How could you embarrass Jalal in such a manner? Did you not know any better?"

I was terrified now. What was Jalal going to do to me? Different kinds of thoughts and scenarios entered my mind. I was afraid that I had pushed him too far. Was he going to beat me to an inch of my life? What had I done? Oh, why did I listen to Khadija? Tears started streaming down my face; I was petrified of the consequences. My poor daughter will suffer because of me. I thanked God that she was with Jalal's aunt, who was a kindhearted woman.

I was stunned when suddenly Jalal backhanded Khadija across the face. She fell to the ground. He looked at her with murder in his eyes. She automatically got to her feet, a look of utter shock entering her eyes.

"Do you know what your jealousy nearly caused, you malicious bitch?"

Cradling her face in her hand, she cried out in pain, "What are you talking about? Are you protecting this infidel? I am your true wife. The one you loved first. You choose me out of all the women in the world."

Jalal laughed at her comment. "My first love, you say. You are an idiot if you believe that. You were a young widow with a son, and I married you, because your family brainwashed me into believing that it was my duty to protect the widowed wife of a martyr. I treated you as a queen, and I even took it upon myself to treat your spoiled son as if he were mine. I married your childless widowed cousin to give her a home to live in. How do you repay my kindness? You tried to get me and the woman I love killed. Your malice knows no bounds. I have pandered to your whims to keep the peace in my family."

I have never heard him talk to Khadija in this manner. I thought she could do no wrong in his eyes. It was a revelation to me. I was shocked by the conversation going on. I always thought that Khadija's son was Jalal's son. Jalal treated him as a son. He was a spoiled brat. He was cocky, and Khadija doted on him. I hated that kid. He was sneaky and had a vicious temper, bullying and striking his sisters. He had no respect for any female figure in the family. I was terrified of him. What was going on in this family? The more secrets were revealed, the more complex they appeared. What power did Khadija have over Jalal? She seemed to dominate this family. I was starting to realize that her power must come from somewhere. What does she have on Jalal that made him concede to her wishes? Where was the monster I thought I had married?

Taking a deep breath, Jalal continued in his rant.

"Khadija, you have overestimated your influence over me. Your family is not as powerful as you think. You have blackmailed me long enough. You have contributed to destroying everything I have held dear to my heart. My family members were hostages to your whims. I have had it with you. The buck stops here."

Khadija looked at Jalal mockingly.

"What are you going to do, tough guy? One word from me, and your whole family would be thrown in prison. Did you forget who my family is? Did you forget how much my father and brothers adore me? Do not dare raise your voice to me. I let you have your fun with this whore. I even turned a blind eye when she gave birth to your bastard daughter. I did this to appease you. Do you think you frighten me?"

Before she could continue with her outburst, Jalal grabbed her by her hair and, in a threatening voice, said, "Do not ever call my daughter a bastard. Do you hear me? The only bastard I see here is you, Khadija. My daughter is my life. I talked to my mother this morning, and she understands your lies. She took all my daughters to my aunt Samira because she loves them. They are safe with her."

I felt relief, knowing my beloved daughter was away from this vicious woman. At least I knew she would be safe.

"Furthermore," continued Jalal, "you and your precious son need to be put in place. The abuse stops here. My daughters are being abused every day. Do you think I do not see how you treat them? Your son has become a monster."

He then shoved her to the ground. Undeterred by his actions, Khadija looked at him with defiance and said, "Think before you throw any more accusations at me. I am not as tolerant as you might think. If you dare abuse me, I will retaliate, and you would not like it one bit."

Laughing hysterically, she continued in a shrill voice: "I want your whore punished for breaking the law. I will laugh and rejoice when she is punished in public."

Turning a murderous look at me, she said in an exceptionally low voice, "My family will hear of this, Jalal. Mark my words. Heads are going to roll. I am not going to spare anyone from my wrath. I will not be humiliated. Do you hear me? I am the daughter of righteous Muslim parents. She is a whore. A disgusting infidel. She is only good for one thing."

Jalal tried to stem her virulent speech, but Khadija did not heed him. A deranged look entered her eyes. I realized that Khadija was not normal. She was mentally unstable. I was so frightened. I had never seen anyone like that. If looks could kill, then I would have perished on the spot. The situation was so surreal.

She continued raving and threatening everyone in Jalal's family.

"I will throw every member of your family in prison. I will sell your daughters into slavery. They are nothing but brats anyway. Even this child in my belly will be put to death. I hate them all. I already negotiating their marriage to righteous men of the faith. Do you think they matter? Only my beloved so matters. He is the chosen one. He will lead this nation one day. All will fall on their knees before him. This child in my belly is also a girl. She means nothing to me. Another mouth to feed. You cannot beget anything with daughters. Unlike my first husband, who is a true man. It says a lot about a man who cannot father a son."

Shaking his head in despair, Jalal looked Khadija straight in the eyes and smiled. Nothing was getting through to her.

"Did you recently talk to your beloved family, Khadija?"

Looking alarmed, Khadija replied, "No, I have not spoken to them in a while. Why are you being so calm about it? When my family hears about this, they will have your head for it, make no mistake."

"Khadija, your father and brothers have all been apprehended. Your esteemed, devoted father and brothers were caught smuggling drugs into Mosul. They were executed today. Your mother and other family members fled Mosul. I helped them escape, and they are now in Rojava, in Kurdish-controlled territory."

Khadija looked shocked.

"You are lying to me. I do not believe you. My father and brothers are devout, righteous individuals. They are the best people in this world. God chose them to be disciples of the faith. How dare you accuse them of such things? This is blasphemy."

"Devout and righteous you say. They were thugs who bullied and harassed everyone around them. They raped young girls for pleasure. They had Yazidi girls enslaved for their pleasure. Their wives forced the Yazidi girls to clean and cook. They beat and starved them constantly. They went to the market and brought Yazidi girls to rape them at home. Some of these girls were as young as thirteen. Your son followed in their footsteps. They took him to the market and bought a girl for him. He raped the poor girl to death."

"Stop right there!" Khadija screamed at Jalal. "It is said in the Quran, and I quote to you, my dear husband, 'O Prophet! We have made lawful to thee thy wives to whom thou hast paid their dowers; and those [slaves] whom thy right hand possesses out of the prisoners of war whom Allah has assigned to the Quran [33:50].

"So they had every right to these unworthy, infidel Yazidi girls. They were following in the steps of our beloved prophet. These infidel women have no rights whatsoever. They are properties of us believers. God gave us the right to abuse those who reject the true faith. We are the chosen ones. These people are nothing but animals. We are superior to everyone."

"Are you serious? Do you believe that these are the actions of devoted Muslims? Do you even understand what that means? Our beloved prophet would never condone such actions. They are a disgrace. I can never love or respect a person such as you. The only protection you have is me. Do not upset me any further. From this day forward, you will not leave the house.

"Everyone thought I married you for love. What a joke. I was blackmailed into it. The only good thing that came out of my marriage to you was my two daughters. I had to pretend I love you to save my family. I was brainwashed into believing this is a just cause. My family tried to show me the error of my ways, but I was blinded by my zeal for this heretic ideology.

"I have become a monster. I do not recognize myself anymore. I am so ashamed of myself. I have abused my wife and family. You are disgusting person. You are sick in the head. I think you need to be institutionalized. I realize now that you were abused as a child. Your parents did a number on you. They brainwashed you with all these false, fundamental ideas. Your first husband was a nutcase. Do you know how abusive and bad he was? Killing and raping his enemies."

Khadija collapsed on the floor, crying and lamenting. Suddenly, she looked at Jalal and screamed.

"You are lying!. You have become an infidel. I am going to report you to the religious police. Just wait, you bastard. You will all executed publicly. I will dance on your grave. The Umma will rise again and conquer the world. The golden age of Islam is close at hand."

Khadija started laughing hysterically like a person possessed. There was an unholy light in her eyes. My body was shivering with fear. I was convinced Khadija was deranged.

"I am going to kill this baby I carry. I am going to kill all your daughters!" she screamed. "They are tainted by your traitorous blood. How dare you treat me this way. I am the daughter of a great man. The follower of the prophet. My deceased husband is a martyr.

He shed his blood on the battleground to free our people of infidel oppression. My son is the only pure blood here. You disgust me. You hear? My son is going to kill you and your whole family. Just wait and see. My father and brothers will kill you and drink your blood. Your beloved infidel wife and daughters will be sold into slavery. You consider yourself a man. You could not even father a son to carry on your legacy. All you have are daughters. Useless daughters who bring shame to our families. Only a real man fathers sons. Your masculinity should be questioned."

Her ranting kept getting crazier and crazier. Jalal tried to reason with her.

"Listen, Khadija, your father and brothers were put to death. They cannot help you. Your whole family is persona non grata."

Khadija could not comprehend what he was saying and kept screaming and shouting threats.

"Stop with your lies and deceit! Do you think I will believe a person such as you? Where is my beloved son? Where is Hamoudi, my son? He is my pride and joy. He will grow up in the image of his father and avenge this disgrace visited upon. You and your whore are trying to hurt me and my family. I will not allow it."

"Khadija, just stop with your ranting and listen very carefully," Jalal said. "Your father and brothers are gone. They will never come back. They have harmed enough people. They were nothing but thugs. Do you hear me? As for your beloved son Hamoudi, he has fled the area. It seems he was caught drinking and taking drugs. He raped an innocent child. She died from her wounds. No one said anything because they considered her an infidel. He is a monster. I rue the day he came into my life. Like father, like son. I do not know where he is, nor do I care. All he did was harass and hurt people. He was an unpleasant boy."

"What did you do with my beloved son? I do not believe what you are saying. He is only sixteen years old. I had dreams of him becoming a martyr like his dad. You killed my son, you murderer. It is his right to take pleasure with any slave girl. God and the prophet had permitted this. Has your great love for this whore blinded you to the truth of our faith?"

"Quran [4:24]: 'And all married women (are forbidden unto you) save those (captives) whom your right hands possess.' Even sex with married slaves is permissible." Khadija recited a verse of the Quran to prove her point.

"I did no such thing, Khadija. I do not forget my religion. I am a devoted Muslim and will always be one. Allah is merciful and does not condone such acts. Stop picking and choosing verses from our holy book. You do not understand the real essence of our faith. Our beloved prophet asked us to treat all people mercifully. He did not want us to become monsters who hurt people."

"As for Hammoudi, you spoiled him rotten. He thought he could do no wrong. How many times have I bailed him out of trouble? I did this in the hope that he would change. I am disgusted by his actions. Raping a child to death without remorse. What have you been teaching him? He is a pedophile. I dare not have him near my daughters. He genuinely believes he can do no wrong. If he had raped your daughters, would that be acceptable? Your father and brothers thought they were indestructible and committed treason. They thought they could overthrow the existing leader and impose themselves as caliphs. They were captured and put to death as traitors to the caliphate."

"My son can do no wrong. He is a good boy destined for greatness. One day he will lead the Umma. You are persecuting my son. You are jealous of him because his father was a great man. You are nothing but an imitation of him. Do not ever say anything bad about my son. As for my daughters, they are nothing to me. They were born to serve Hammoudi. They have no rights. Their brother is their lord and master. If he wanted to take them to bed, that is his right. He is superior to any girl. Anyway, did you see how your daughters tried to seduce him? They are whores."

Jalal slapped Khadija hard. "You are a disgusting human being. You would condone a brother raping his sisters. You are an animal. Our daughters are still children, and you claim they are trying to seduce their brother. You are one sick individual. Hammoudi is nothing but a menace to humanity. He tortured my daughters and hurt them. As for your esteemed first husband, he was nothing but a thug. He blew himself up in a school, killing innocent children. Is that the action of a good, compassionate man? Just stop with all this nonsense. I think you are unhinged."

Khadija suddenly collapsed on the floor, mumbling under her breath, "Hammoudi, my beloved son, where are you? Hammoudi, come and help me."

Shaking his head, Jalal grabbed Khadija and dragged her to her room. He locked the door behind her.

Tina, the Love of My Life, Please Forgive Me

He looked at me and then fell to his knees in front of me.

"Tina, forgive me."

"What did you call me, Jalal?" I was shocked to my core. Jalal asking for my forgiveness. Jalal kneeling in front of me, calling me Tina. I was in disbelief. How did this happen?

"I called you Tina, my love, my heart, my soul."

"But you made me change my name. You thought Tina was an infidel name."

"I met you as Tina, I fell in love with you as Tina, you would always be Tina for me. Can you ever forgive for the abhorrent way I have treated you? I was an idiot, brainwashed by a fundamental movement that has no relation to any form of religion. I had no right to force you to change our name or religion. I have lied to you all through our relationship. I could not show you how much I loved you. Khadija was always there watching me. Her power over me was absolute. I have finally broken her hold over me. I finally realized she is unbalanced."

He grabbed my hands and started kissing them. Tears were streaming down his face.

"I have shown you little love, affection, or compassion throughout our marriage. I have abused you mentally and physically. I treated you crueler than my worst enemy. I was possessed with hate, jealousy, and bitterness. If it takes the rest of my life, I will try to make it up to you."

I could not contain myself. I burst into tears.

"Please, my love, stop crying. I know what I have done. What I have become. A monster with no conscience. I do not know how you can even tolerate looking at me. Can you ever forgive me? I forced you to do horrible things. I have alienated you from your family, culture, and friends. I wanted you all for myself. Khadija knew how obsessed I was with you. She did her best to hurt you. She used my jealousy and love for you to hurt you. No matter how much I say, I cannot justify my actions toward you. You are perfect.

"I threatened you with the most heinous acts. I belittled you. Cast you as a villain. I used your love of our daughter against you. I threatened to sell her to the highest bidder. I also threatened to give you to my men. I have no defense for my actions."

Before Jalal could continue with his wallowing in guilt, I put my hand up. "Please stop your speech. I cannot take any more of this. I know you feel guilty, but what you put me through cannot be forgiven easily. I have been to hell with you. You abused me both mentally and physically. You made a mockery of my love for you. I left all that was dear for you. I alienated myself from loved ones for you. I converted to Islam for you. Changed my name, my identity for you. I sacrificed my life for you, and what did I get back in return? Nothing but hatred and abuse. You say you loved me. Please spare me from such love. If it were not for my beloved daughter, I would have killed you and myself a long time ago. I do not want to hear any of this. I cannot and will not trust you anymore."

While talking tears were streaming down my face. I started sobbing as if my heart has been broken.

Jalal looked like a broken man. He did not know what to say.

"Tina, listen to me I know. What I did was wrong."

"Please, Jalal, just stop!" I screamed. "I cannot listen to your excuses. Do you think you can turn back time and change everything? Can you give me my life back? What have I ever done to you to treat me this way?"

"I know you have sacrificed a lot for me—"

Interrupting him, I said, "*Sacrificed*, you say? How about giving my whole life for you. I loved you so much that you became my life. I endured abuse from your wife and children. You lied to me about being married. You not only had one wife but two. You tell me, how I can ever overlook that? I have already been sentenced to fifty lashes in public."

"Listen to me, Tina, do not be frightened. I talked to the people in power. They are not going to administer your punishment. They understand the situation."

"People in power, you say. Your dear friends who have made my life a living hell with their laws and religion."

I was livid. I had enough of this farce. Jalal had a change of heart, and I was supposed to forgive him? How could I? I had been treated worse than an animal. My dignity was shredded to pieces. I did not how I survived this long. I did not know. My family back home had my best interest at heart, and I completely shut them out. For what? I wondered. To live in this hell with a man who nearly destroyed me. I could not turn the other cheek anymore. I have reached my limit. Jalal might be sorry, but it was too little too late. I did not have it to even care about his needs. He wanted absolution from his heinous deeds. I could not give it to him. I was a broken woman, but I knew one thing for sure—I wanted to get out of this hellhole, and I needed his help. I could not bring myself to trust this new Jalal.

It was too much for me. Jalal had done things that were unforgivable. I knew he loved me, but I could do without this love. How could he even imagine that I could ever forgive him? He was a monster, and no matter how much he tried to make it up to me, it would never be enough. He had brought me to this hellhole. He put me and my precious daughter in danger. My life could never be the same. I had become a shell of my former self. How could he even think that I could ever forgive him for that? My love for him had turned to hatred. I could not fathom how much my feelings had changed so much. I realized my capacity for making excuses for me was at an end. I had nothing left in me to give him. I had loved him with all my heart. I made excuses for every horrible action he had committed, but this time I could not find it in myself to even care what he thought or did. As far as I was concerned, it was over.

Khadija Is No More

Suddenly I heard a loud bang from Khadija's bedroom. Both Jalal and I ran toward the room to see what was going on. The moment I entered the room, a grisly sight met my eyes. Khadija had hung herself with a shawl from the ceiling fan. Her body was swinging around with the fan. Jalal ran to her and tried to cut her loose, but it was too late. She had killed herself and her unborn child. She had taken the ultimate revenge on Jalal. She had killed his unborn child.

I heard screaming, not realizing that it was me. I continued to scream, and my screams became louder. I could not stop myself. Jalal gathered me close, trying to shield me from seeing her unmoving body. My mind could not take anymore, and I fainted in Jalal's arms. After that I did not know what happened.

When I came back to my senses, I was in bed in Jalal's bedroom. It was early morning. It was the first time I had ever slept in Jalal's bedroom. Samira was sleeping in a chair next to my bed, and my daughter was snuggled next to me. Suddenly all that had happened came rushing back, and I started screaming. Samira woke to my screams, and my infant daughter started crying. Samira took me in her arms and started soothing me.

Your Daughter Needs You

"My dear, you need to get yourself together. Calm down. Your daughter needs you. Please, sweetie, calm down. You cannot have a breakdown at this time. Who will take care of your family? Honey, please calm down."

Finally, after a while, I calmed down. My daughter's pathetic cries brought me back to my senses. What was going to happen now? I was so confused. I picked my crying daughter in my arms and started to sooth her.

"Amira, my love. Calm down, sweetie. Everything is going to be okay. Mommy is here. My love, please calm down."

Eventually, my daughter fell asleep, still crying. I hugged her to my breast, and tears were streaming from my eyes. I knew deep down in my heart that I needed to be strong for her. My aim in life was getting away from this hellhole that I was in. I wanted to go back home. See my parents' faces and go down on my knees, asking them for their forgiveness. I wanted to rip my veil off and walk free down the streets in my parents' neighborhood. I wanted to be free of this terror. I wanted my daughter to experience freedom and be surrounded by loved ones.

I put my daughter down on the bed and looked up to see that Samira was still in the room.

Tina, Please Forgive Me

"Sweetie, please listen to me. I know you are upset."

"Upset? Upset, you say? More like traumatized. I am entitled to some hysteria, don't you agree? Stop with your platitudes. Your nephew is a monster. He has destroyed so many lives. He marries me under false pretentions, drags me to this godforsaken country, threatens and abuses me, and I should forgive him? Because he said he loves me? Give me a break. I hate him, his family, and everything relating to him. I hate him, I hate him, do you hear me? I will never forgive him. Never. Never. Leave me alone. Just leave me alone. You and your entire family can go to hell for all I care."

Samira looked at me with shock and hurt. I knew she was always kind to me and tried to protect me and my child, but I could not forget that she was related to that monster who called himself my husband. She had unwillingly participated in deceiving me. I was so emotionally scared that I could not reason. I knew she meant well, but I did not have it in me to look kindly on her or her help.

"I am so sorry, Tina, I truly I am."

"All of a sudden you all remember my name," I cried out in pain. "You and your family tried to destroy my identity. You all called me Aisha for the longest time. I nearly forgot who I was. Can you imagine someone erasing your history, your identity, and your culture? This is what you guys do. You have no respect for different cultures or identities. All you do is destroy other people's identity and impose your views and religion on them. You are all monsters. Monsters, I tell you. Just leave me alone. I have had as much as anyone can take from you. Leave, just leave." By this point I was shouting at her. I knew I was repeating myself continually, but I was furious with the situation I was forced into. I was bereft of further thoughts or words. My ranting had become repetitive, but I could not help myself. I was finally able to express my true feelings. The floodgates were open at last. I could not contain the viral words coming out of my mouth.

Finally, Samira stood and left the room. I sat in the empty bedroom, save for my daughter who slept peacefully, unaware of the turmoil going on around her. My life was falling to pieces. I did not know what to do. I felt exhausted both physically and mentally. I was at the end of my tether. What was I supposed to do now? I was terrified of the repercussions of Khadija's actions. Where they going to come after Jalal now? Deep down, I knew that he was the only one who could protect me. I was not so far gone that I did not realize that fact. I needed him to help me escape this place. He was my only hope. This last thought terrified me. What if he could not let me go? I knew that the ruling bodies did not allow anyone to leave their territory. They wanted complete control of the populace. They prohibited any travel outside of their control. I also knew that Jalal had many connections to the outside world. He was able to smuggle Khadija's mother and sisters to Baghdad. Maybe he could do the same thing for me.

Facing the Truth about Myself

I hear Jalal and Samira whispering in the living room. I also heard sobbing coming from Jalal. I could not believe Jalal was crying. What was he up to? Through my time spent in this house, I had become attuned to the slightest of noises. I inched toward the bed, intending to listen to their conversation. I wanted to know what was going on around me. I did not trust anyone. I needed to find out what was happening on my own. In my mind, they were all my enemy. I needed to depend on myself for everything. Lord have mercy on my soul.

"Nephew, my dear, please stop crying. I know how difficult this is for you."

"Aunt, I have lost a daughter. The bitch killed my child. No matter how much I hated Khadija, I loved my unborn child. She was innocent of all this mess. How could a mother be so heartless? She killed her own child. Her own child. She killed herself to punish me. She wanted to kill my daughter."

"I have been going through hell with her. She has been abusing her daughters since they were little children. I was kept busy protecting them from her and her despicable son. When I met Tina, she saw a way to control me further. I was going to divorce her and marry Tina when she changed her tactics. She begged me to stay married to her. She promised me that she will do all she can to help Tina become accustomed to our culture. She promised me to be a good wife to me and take good care of our daughters. She was an ideal person. She knew I did not love her. She played me like a fiddle. I believed her. From the beginning she was hateful toward Tina. She treated Tina well in front of me, but the minute my back was turned the abuse started."

Sobbing, Jalal continued his story. "Khadija brainwashed my mother against Tina. She painted a picture of a loose, grasping woman getting her hooks into a married man. She manipulated the whole family. She played on my jealousies and insecurities to get her way. Her family was powerful, and she threatened to destroy my family back here in Mosul. I became so paranoid, I treated Tina badly. I destroyed her love for me. I blame myself for all this. I should have left Tina alone. I fell in love with her at first sight. She was honest and earnest in her desire to change the world for the better. I played on her innocence to get her to fall in love with me. She cut ties with all her family and friends to appease me. What did I do to repay her? I abused and belittled her. I pray to God Almighty to forgive me. Aunt, I love her so much. I do not want to lose her."

"Listen, Jalal, it is not all your fault. Tina played a huge role in this. She played right into your hands. If she knew her own mind and was loyal to her beliefs, all this would not have happened. She thought she knew everything. She alienated herself from her family. If she genuinely loved her family, nothing could have separated her from them. I am not making excuses for your actions. They were despicable, but let us look at things from all angles. You did not force her to do anything. She wanted to follow you. She converted to Islam and followed your edicts."

"What do you mean, Auntie? What are you hinting at?"

"Do not take my words the wrong way. I am worried about Tina. She is in a bad way. She is distraught over everything going on. I fear she might hurt herself. She is a good and virtuous woman. I do not know why you have treated her so badly. She has been through a lot. I do not know how you can ever make it up to her. But let me tell you something important. Tina is not innocent in all this scenario. She brought this situation upon herself. She rejected her beliefs and culture. She treated her family horribly. She even threatened to call the authorities on them. No matter the situation, you do not treat your parents in such a manner. I understand she thought she was doing the right thing, but her parents were good people. They loved her so much. They were always good to her. Her betrayal runs deep."

Hearing Samira say that, I was struck to my core. She was right. I was not a good and virtuous person. I treated my family very badly. I betrayed and abused them. My shame went deep. How can I take the moral high ground when I was a betrayer? I now understand the anguish and hurt my family went through. How can I forgive myself? They wanted the best for me. Can I imagine my daughter, my own flesh and blood, treating me the way I treated my own parents and brothers? While musing on all my failings, Samira continued in her questioning of Jalal's situation.

"How are you going to proceed from here? What is going to happen? Have the authorities been notified of Khadija's suicide? Where are your daughters?"

"Aunt, please calm down. I will tell you everything when the right time comes. Believe me, everything will become clear in a couple of weeks. At present, I need to grieve for my daughter. No matter how much I resented Khadija for her actions, I loved my daughter. She was innocent in all this. Her conception was not ideal. Khadija drugged me and seduced me into her bed. I have not shared her bed for years. She knew how to hurt me. She did it through her pregnancy."

"Okay, my beloved nephew, remember that I am here for you. I know it is not the ideal time now, but you need to think of ways of getting out of here before everything blows up in our faces. The world and the Iraqi government are not going to let this situation go much further. They are going to retake Mosul and drive ISIS out. The situation has been desperate. People are hungry. Food prices have rocketed through the roof. In addition, I heard that there was some resistance within Mosul, but they were ruthlessly crushed. People are being detained all the time for the slightest infractions. Society is collapsing. I am old and will not leave my beloved city, but you need to make plans to get out of here. You have many connections, use them to get your wife and daughters out of here. Please think hard. You might have no other choice."

119

Jalal Reassessing His Beliefs

"I am extremely disappointed with the whole situation. I was such an idealist. Thinking everything will be better with the implementation of the Sharia. I had no idea what I was advocating for. I saw how bad the Shia government was treating us, and I wanted to help our people. I was so blinded by my idealism that I destroyed all that was good and pure in me. I married a woman who made my life hell. I took her and her son under my wing and thought I can change the world. How stupid could I have been?

"Aunt Samira, I need time to come to grips with all that is going on. The authorities were notified of her death, and they think that she went off the rails after the death of her brothers and father. They had no sympathy for her. In their eyes she is considered a sinner. They refused to give her a proper burial. I had to bribe someone to give her a proper burial. Even though she made my life hell, she was still my wife and mother of my daughters."

"My beloved nephew, we were all praying that you would see the light. I am so glad that you have finally broken the shackles that bind you. These people are pure evil. There is nothing good about them. This is not Islam. It is a corrupted version of their interpretation of our religion. The only real problem here is your relationship with Tina. You lied and deceived her, it is true, but your treatment of her was abhorrent. I know she brought a lot on her with her blind devotion to you and stubbornness, but I cannot help but feel that your marriage can never be mended."

Jalal nodded in agreement. It was the first time I had ever seen him in such a state. He looked pale and sick and so unsure of himself.

Tears were streaming down his face. He was not the man I knew. His pain and vulnerability were evident. He was always confidant and sure of his beliefs. I always thought that he never questioned himself. This new Jalal was an enigma to me. What can I say to such a man? I was scared to death. At least with the old Jalal I knew where I stood.

I cleared my throat, and both Samira and Jalal turned toward me.

"Are you okay, Tina?" Jalal asked.

"As fine as anyone can be in this situation. What do you expect me to say, Jalal, that it is all fine and dandy?'

"I know, Tina, I understand your hatred and resentment toward me."

I shook my head at him. "Jalal you need to understand something. At this moment I am operating on autopilot. I do not have much feeling for you one way or another. My emotions are depleted. The only thing I care about is my daughter and finding a way to get out of this hellhole I find myself in. I want to go home."

Jalal cast his eyes to the floor and nodded. "Tina, I am going to do all that I can to get us out of this situation that I brought onto our heads. I promise you this. To my last dying breath, I shall protect you and my children."

Taking a deep breath, Jalal continued, "I need you to promise me one thing, Tina. It is the only thing I will ever ask of you."

"What is it, Jalal?"

"If I do not make it out alive, will you take my daughters with you back to the USA? I know it is a lot to ask of you in this situation, but they do not have anyone else. I know I do not deserve this promise, but I beg you with all my heart to take care of them. They have no one else. My family is scattered all over and can barely look after themselves, and Khadija's family is a mess. I do not want my daughters anywhere near them."

"But I am the Christian infidel whore. The person you degraded so badly. You yourself said that I needed to be grateful to have converted to Islam. I am not worthy of taking care of your precious daughters. Do not ask this of me. I no longer believe in anything you believe. I refute you and your horrible religion. I thought I was doing the world a great favor by converting. Little did I know what I was getting myself into."

"Tina, I beg you, lower your voice. Do you understand what you are saying? If anyone even suspects what you say, they will kill you. Apostasy is punishable by death in Islam."

"And you consider yourselves the true religion. Killing anyone who disagrees with you. This says it all. I am officially in hell."

"Tina, I am sorry for the way I have treated you, but I am still a devoted Muslim. I will not allow you to disparage my faith. I know I have done many bad things, but this does not mean you have the right to attack my faith. Do you understand?"

"I perfectly understand, my dear husband. You can insult me and insult my beliefs, but I cannot even mention what I feel."

"You forgot something vital in our relationship, Tina. You yourself rejected your own beliefs. You turned your back on your culture and beliefs. You insulted and demeaned your friends and family. I never made you do anything you did not want to do. I am not putting the blame all on you. I pursued you with all I had. I cannot lie to you, but did I insult you family? Take some responsibility for your actions. You were ripe for the plucking. You thought you knew everything. It was quite easy to manipulate you and mold you into the person I wanted you to be."

His words stopped me dead in my tracks. He was right. I had brought all this situation on myself. I was not going to dwell on this anymore. I needed to look forward and get out of the mess I currently found myself in.

"Furthermore, Tina, this is not the time and place for recrimination. We need to plan carefully for our escape. I cannot keep worrying about your erratic behavior. I understand you have been through a lot, but I do not have the time to appease you. I have just lost a daughter, who I need to grieve. Two daughters who lost their mother. Even though Khadija was a lousy mother, she was still their mother. They need all our support. They are two innocent young girls. Do not turn away from them, Tina. I beg you. We can only get out of here if we stick together."

Turning to Samira, he said, "Aunt I need you and your husband to bring my daughters home. I love you, and the only way to protect you is to not see you. I need to plan very carefully our next move. I still have contacts with the government in Baghdad. I will do my best to get us out of here. The authorities here trust and think I was dealt a bad hand from Khadija and her family. They are sympathetic to my situation. I will play on their sympathy and show my loyalty to them, until I have a plan to escape this cursed place. I do not want your family to be suspect of anything."

"I understand, my love. I am so relieved that you have finally opened your eyes to the truth. Our family has been praying for a long time for you to see the truth. Hamdallah for this miracle. Remember, my dearest nephew, we love you. Do not worry about us. We are capable of taking care of ourselves. As for you, Tina, I am sorry for all that you have been through. Remember, we love and respect you. I know you were treated badly by my nephew, but he genuinely loves you."

With that, she called her husband, who was waiting for her in another room with Jalal's two daughters. The girls were innocently sleeping in the room. They did not know what had happened. It was left to us to give them the news of their mother and brother. It was a daunting task. Samira and her husband left. As they left, I felt as if I had lost a family member. Samira and her husband were among the few who were kind to me.

United for a Common Cause

. . . .

"Listen, Tina, we need to be on the same page here. You cannot keep fighting me. I am only human. There is only so much I can tolerate. I realize my behavior toward you has been atrocious, but you must snap out of your hatred and resentment of me if we want to get out of this situation in one piece. Do you understand what I am saying?"

"Yes, Jalal, I understand. I will do everything you tell me. I know you are my only hope of surviving this."

"Thank you, Tina."

"We need to plan our strategy very carefully. Daish leaders are not stupid. Eventually, they will figure out what we are up to. I cannot call you Tina anymore. The walls have ears. Their spies are everywhere. We need to continue with the charade of being loyal citizens of the Islamic State."

"Tell me what I need to do, and I will do it."

"The less you know now, the better. I will figure everything out and let you know. I need to get in contact with old allies outside the city and find a way of escaping."

"I will put all my trust in you, Jalal, but I need to ask you something."

"What is it? If it is in my power, I will grant it."

"If we get out of here alive, I want a divorce."

"Tina, you are asking me to rip my heart out of my chest. Ask me again when we get out of here."

"Thank you, Jalal."

"I have a request of my own."

"What is it?"

"Promise me to take care of my girls if something happens to me. Before saying anything, listen carefully to me. They are innocent in all that Khadija and I did. They acted badly toward you because they were egged on by their vicious mother. Do not hold their childish behavior against them."

"I promise, Jalal, I will take care of them." These kids were innocent. They did not know right from wrong. I promised myself that I would teach them to be better human beings. Then I thought to myself that I needed to be a better human being. There were so many fences to mend if I ever returned home. I quickly rejected that negative thought. I will return home. I wanted to hug my parents and brothers and beg for their forgiveness. There was no place in my life for failure. Nothing was going to stop me from achieving my goal.

I also knew that no matter how remorseful Jalal was, I could never fully accept him as my husband. I knew deep down inside that he was the biggest mistake of my life. We were two vastly different people, from different cultures and belief systems. I could not play second fiddle to him anymore. My naive assumptions of love conquering all have crumbled. I could not change who I was. I did not have a subservient personality. I had repressed myself to fit in, but all that would stop once I was back home. I was proud of my background and heritage; I refuse to discard it to appease anyone. Lord, give me strength.

"Promise me on the soul of our beloved daughter, Aisha."

"I promise, Jalal." I just realized how vulnerable Jalal was. He was terrified for his beloved family. I could not fault him for that. He was a good father. As he said, I could not hold their childish behavior against them.

Suddenly, I realized that my mother-in-law was not in the house. "Where is your mother, Jalal?"

"My mother is so ashamed of her behavior toward you that she left and is staying at my aunt Samira's house."

"I forgive her, Jalal. She is an old woman and needs to be with her son."

"I know that, sweetie, but she is a stubborn old woman. She refuses to listen to me. She does not want to leave Mosul and honestly believes her place is with my aunt. Nothing will change her mind. She only prays that one day things will improve in our beloved country. She is very ill and has weeks to live. The doctors have warned her to take it easy and relax. She knows she will not live long. I will go and visit her soon. I do not want to endanger you or my daughters. It is tough, but this is how it will be. She asks you to forgive her."

"I do, Jalal. I hold no animosity toward her. She was blinded by Khadija. Bring her here, let me take care oof her."

"She is in the last stages of lung cancer. The doctors believe she will not last more than a couple of weeks."

"Please, Jalal, bring her home. Let her die in her home."

"I will try. Maybe she can make her peace with you."

With that said, Jalal left the house to go collect his mother.

Death of Jalal's Mother

It had been two weeks since that fateful day Khadija committed suicide. Last night Jalal's mother died peacefully in her sleep. Thank God her suffering was over. Jalal, with some of his relatives, took her body to be buried. Only men were allowed at the burial site. In accordance with Muslim traditions, the dead needed to be buried within twenty-four hours of their passing.

We made our peace at last. She asked for my forgiveness, and I readily gave it. She had also asked me to forgive Jalal for his actions. She was so contrite over the way things panned out. Finally, she was at peace. Samira came over to prepare her for burial. She was staying with me and the children until Jalal came back. She was a great help. I was grateful for all the support she showed me during my time here. I could not have withstood all that was happening without her.

Jalal's daughters, Rima and Sahar, were becoming my shadow. After the nightmare of their mother's death, they latched on to me. They were starved for attention and kindness. They competed for my bidding. They adored their little sister, Amira. I was shocked by their behavior. I thought they hated and resented me. It seemed Khadija had threatened to beat them up if they were nice to me. I was shocked by how much these little girls had suffered. They did not ask about their older brother, Hammoundi. They told me how terrified they were of him. He would beat them and threaten them all the time.

How things have changed in these two weeks. Jalal had lost his wife, daughter, and mother. He was putting on a good front, but I knew he was devastated. He had a lot on his mind. He was planning our escape but was worried about being found out. He would be automatically executed, and I would be given to another man as a slave. I also knew our children would be married off to the soldiers of the Islamic State. I was terrified of this. When I asked Jalal the reasoning behind this, he said while quoting Sahih Bukhari (62:137): "An account of women taken as slaves in battle by Muhammad's men after their husbands and fathers were killed. The woman were raped with Muhammad's approval."

I was disgusted with such a quote, but Jalal told me this was not part of the Quran and that Daish tried to justify their actions with quotes taken out of context. As far as he was concerned, their actions did not reflect the heart of the Muslim faith.

We did not say anything in front of the kids, fearing anyone questioning them. We behaved normally. We did not even talk to each other about our potential escape. We knew that the walls had ears. ISIL officials were becoming paranoid. They were squashing anyone they thought was opposing them. Their brutality knew no bounds. Bodies littered the streets of Mosul. The situation was becoming desperate. Food and essential products were becoming scarce. It was frightening. People queued for hours to get bread and water.

Jalal still attended meeting with the state's officials, but I knew he was plotting for our escape. Jalal had been in contact with the Baghdad government. He was giving them intel on the Islamic State. I also knew that the Iraqi government was planning to retake Mosul. We needed to get out before the attack.

Jalal finally returned home from the burial. Samira left with her husband. Jalal asked me to pray with him.

"I know that you have lost your faith, but can you try and pray with me in memory of my mother?"

I could not refuse his request. I changed, cleaned myself, and changed my clothes to pray with him. After prayer I prepared a small meal, and we ate our meal with the children. After we put the children to bed, Jalal asked me to sit down because he had something to discuss with me.

"It is time, Tina. I have everything set. I have bribed smugglers to get us out."

Upon hearing this, my heart started fluttering. I was excited at the prospect of getting out of Mosul.

"Listen to me, Tina, we might not get out of this alive, but we need to try. It is going to be dangerous, but I do not think we have any other option."

"I understand, Jalal, but I will do anything to get out of here."

"I have bribed a truck driver who is sympathetic with our plight to smuggle us out of Mosul in a gas tanker."

It was our only option. Jalal was a well-known face among the ISIL leadership. He needed to get out of this, or the game would be over.

Our Escape

Our escape from Mosul was anticlimactic. Things went smoothly. We bundled the girls up at midnight and left the apartment. Fearing the girls might make noise and give us away, we gave them some sleeping pills. A close friend and ally of Jalal helped us get to the appointed place where the oil tanker was parked. We got inside the tanker and waited until dawn when the curfew was lifted. I was terrified of the slightest noise. Jalal, wanting to help me with my anxiety, gave me some pills to relax me. Little did I know that they were sleeping pills. I went to sleep and was woken up when Jalal roughly shook me awake.

"Wake up, Tina, we have escaped Mosul. We are at the Iraqi checkpoint. We need to get out."

I was terrified that the Iraqi army would take us into custody.

"Are you not afraid that they will harm us?" I cried in fear. "What if they kill you. What would I do?"

"Calm down, Tina. I have already been in touch with the American and Iraqi forces. They are expecting us."

The girls woke up groggy, upset, and hungry. Amira started crying and would not stop. I was at my wits' end. The girls were terrified. An official came and took us into a makeshift office twenty meters away from the checkpoint. They left me and the girls there and took Jalal away. The girls were all crying, and I could not console them. I changed Amira and fed her and gave the girls some bread to calm them down.

Finally, after what seemed like hours, Jalal returned with some officials. At this point I was on the brink of collapse. I was scared, hungry, and exhausted. The girls were cranky and inconsolable. I was in the dark on our fate. Were they going to imprison us, rip the girls from our arms, torture us? Different scenarios were going through my head.

"Tina," Jalal said, "do not worry. All will be well. We have an escort to the American embassy in Irbil. We are going to meet with the American counselor there. I have been in touch with them. They will debrief me, and then I will sign papers giving you full custody of the girls. From Irbil you and the girls will take a flight to Istanbul, and from there you will take a connecting flight back to the USA. Your parents were contacted, and they will meet you at the airport. I will be returning to help the Iraqi Army liberate Mosul."

Sighing deeply, he continued, "I know it is a huge responsibility taking the girls under your wing, but I have no choice in the matter. You need to be strong for them. I trust you. All I ask is that you do not hate me. Remember me with kindness." With that he kissed me on the head, hugged the girls, and departed with his escorts. It was the last time we talked.

American Embassy in Erbil

The girls and I bundled in a waiting car and Jalal in another. After many hours of arduous driving, we arrived at the American consulate. Jalal was met at the door by American military personal and escorted inside. On the other hand, we were escorted into a waiting room by a nice-looking young man. By this time, I had ripped the veil from my head and the niqab from my face. I wanted to feel fear. The girls were being fussy. They were hungry and tired. I felt dirty. Finally, a young woman came and escorted me toward the counselor's office. I entered the office, and a distinguished-looking gentleman was seated behind a desk. When he saw me enter with the girls, he came around the desk and held his hand out to me.

I shook his hand, and he looked at the girls and smiled.

"My name is Jeff. Welcome to our embassy." Looking directly at the girls, he addressed them in a gentle voice.

"Hi, young ladies. Are you hungry? Jeff is here." He gestured to the young man who had escorted us into the office. "Will take you to have some food."

Both girls looked at him strangely. They did not understand English much.

"Girls," I said in Arabic, "please take your sister Amira and go with this nice man. He is going to feed you."

Sahar held Amira in her arms, and they followed the young man out to get some food.

"Madam, I can see you're exhausted from your ordeal. I will be as brief as possible. You and the girls will be taken to a hotel room to rest and get a meal. New clothes for you and the girls will be waiting in your room when you arrive. You can shower and change your clothes. Your husband will be debriefed by our security team and then will be returning to Mosul. You are booked on a plan to Ankara tomorrow, and from Ankara you will fly back to the States. Your parents will meet you at the airport. You need to sign some papers that will give you guardianship of the girls. Do you have any questions?"

"Did you get in touch with my family?"

"Yes, they were relieved you were alive and healthy. They were worried sick about you and your daughter. They will meet you at the airport. I know you have been through a lot, but you need to be strong for your girls. Many people are going to resent you, and you cannot blame them. You need to do much to change your image."

Looking me in the eye, he continued. "I will be honest with you. I did not want you to return to the USA. You have done much damage to our image. In my eyes you are a traitor. You partially redeemed yourself when your husband abandoned ISIS. We promised him to help you return home, and in return he needs to help us in our fight against ISIS."

"I understand what you are saying and am grateful for all your help. I left my family and country for a false promise. I have many regrets. I thank you for all your help."

"Tina, you need to understand your husband can never return to the USA."

"I know, but it makes no difference to me."

"He risked much to escape from Mosul."

"I am thankful for that, but it cannot erase all the lies and deceit that he put me through. I was blinded by his fervor and passion for his beliefs. I gave up everything for him. I changed my religion, disowned my family and friends to earn his love. All I got in return was hurt and lies. I am sorry for sounding bitter, but—"

Jeff interjected, "I understand your sentiments. Say no more. I will call my assistant to take you and the girls to your hotel after you have signed these documents. They were prepared beforehand. Your husband has already signed them. They make you the legal guardian to the girls. I will call my assistant to witness your signature."

After I signed the papers, Jeff said, "My assistant will escort you to your hotel. Rest and take it easy. You have a long journey home. Good luck."

Home Sweet Home

· ·

At long last, I arrived home with my daughter, Amira, and Jalal's two daughters, Rima and Sahar. Amira was held to my breast, and Rima and Sahar clutched to my skirts. I had discarded the veil and niqab. I was finally free with the burden of the last year. I was so overjoyed to be home. My parents met me at the airport. They were hesitant at first. Fearing my reaction to their presence. I ran to them with tears in my eyes, hugging and kissing them. They were crying, kissing, and hugging me at the same time. Amira, not liking to be left out, started screaming. They took her from my arms. She calmed down when they started fussing over her.

"Our beloved Tina. We have missed you. We are so ecstatic to meet our beloved granddaughter. Sweetheart, she is the spitting image of you. She is beautiful. Absolutely beautiful."

I knew my parents were happy that Amira looked like me. I could not blame them. They did not want to be reminded of the man who had taken their daughter from them. I was lost, and finally I have returned to them. Like the prodigal son.

Suddenly, Rima and Sahar, who were hiding behind me, came forth. They came forth and looked at my parents curiously. My parents looked at both girls in shock. I should have told my parents about them. I was afraid my parents might do something that would upset the girls. They were very vulnerable at this stage.

"Mum, Dad," I said, "these two little girls are Rima and Sahar. They are my stepdaughters. I know you do not want anything to remind you of Jalal, but these two little girls are innocent of their parents' sins. I beg you do not turn away from them. They have lost everyone close to them. They have no one in the world but me. They have become dear to my heart."

After the way I had behaved with my parents, I did not expect to get any compassion from them. I did not know what to do or go if my parents refused to take them in.

"I beg you, do not turn away from us. We have nowhere to go. I promise that you will not see or hear them while they are staying with you. They are well-behaved girls and have suffered a lot. They were abused by their mother and older brother. I beseech you, take pity on them."

I grabbed my parents' hands and kissed them. "I have sinned against you in the worst possible way. You gave me the best in life, and I abused your love and turned my back on you. Please forgive me. I have seen the error of my ways. Please, Mum and Dad, forgive me. Do not let my sins cloud your judgment."

I was trembling with shame and fear. My parents were so happy and relieved to see me and their grandkid, but they did not want to be bothered by another person's kids. Especially, a person who had abused and hurt their only daughter. Jalal, in their opinion, had destroyed their family. They did not look kindly on anything related to him. I was crying in earnest, fearing the worst.

My mother enfolded me in her arms, crying hard. My father was also crying.

"Tina, please calm down. We are so happy to see you. We can never turn our back on these kids."

"Sweetie," my father said, "do not worry. We cannot, in fair conscience, turn our back on these kids. Let us go home."

I was relieved to hear what my dad had said. I knew it was going to be hard on everyone involved, but I had little choice in the matter. I had nowhere to go. Besides, I missed my family. I wanted to feel safe and loved. They were a safe harbor in the raging storm that was my life. My mother held my daughter close to her heart and walked us toward their sports utility car. Rima and Sahar followed us closely. They were holding on to me as if their life depended on it. They were trembling from fear. They did not speak or understand English very well, but they knew that they were not wanted. Living with Khadija and her son Hammoudi, these poor girls were sensitive to people's feelings. I wanted to hug them to me and tell them all would be well, but the time was not right.

"Sweetie," my mum said, "you need time to relax and heal from all you have been through before anything can be discussed."

"Thanks, Mum, you do not know how much this means to me. I am exhausted both physically and mentally."

I had little luggage with us. We had fled Mosul with little. I was so grateful to be back home that I did not care about anything else. The nightmare was over. We all bundled into the car. Unfortunately, my parents did not know about Rima and Sahar, so they did not have child seats for them. They had one for my daughter. When we were all strapped in the car, we headed home. I was so exhausted that I and the girls fell asleep all the way home. My parents' home was an hour's drive from the airport.

My mother gently shook me. "Wake up, Tina, we have arrived home."

I opened my eyes and saw my childhood home. It was a dream come true. I was finally home. I felt safe at last.

My parents helped me get the children out of the car and into the house.

"Tina, we have prepared your old room for you and put a cot there for Amira. We will prepare your brother's old room for the girls."

"Mum, thank you for all you have done. I cannot ask for more, but I am afraid the girls will wake up terrified to be alone. They have lost so much. Can I have them with me in my room for now, until they get used to the house?"

"That is fine, my dear. We will get some sleeping bags for them to sleep in."

"That is fine, Mum. I am so sorry for everything. I have no right to ask you for anything."

"Tina, stop your self-flagellation, my dear. You need to feel better before we can talk about all that has happened. This is not the right time or place. We are going to give you space to get better before we can tackle all our personal problems."

"Thanks, Mum. You do not know how much I appreciate you."

"Tina, go take a shower. I have out a change of clothes for you. Your dad has already put Amira in her cot, and the girls are huddled together on your bed."

I showered and went to bed. The girls cuddled to me in their sleep. I fell asleep the minute my head hit the pillow. I woke up the next day, disoriented. Looking around, the girls were not in the room. I started to panic until I remembered I was back home. I got up and dressed in some jeans and T-shirt my mother had left out for me. It was around ten thirty in the morning. I had overslept. I was worried about the girls. They had little clothes. I had some money with me that Jalal had given me before we returned to the States. I wanted to ask my mother if she was willing to take me to a discount store to buy some clothes for the girls.

I headed down to the kitchen. The girls were all sitting around the kitchen table, eating pancakes. My mum was hard at work interacting with all girls. Dad was also there with Amira on his lap. When Rima and Sahar saw me, they jumped up from their chairs and hugged me. They were smiling at me. Their mouths were full of pancakes.

"Mama," they choirused; it was still a bit disconcerting hearing them refer to me by that name. "We thought you will sleep forever. We have been up for ages."

I realized something vital here. Amira, my daughter, was not as clingy as Rima and Sahar. She was content to sit on my father's lap, lapping all the attention. On the other hand, Rima and Sahar wanted me always within their sight. They were terrified I would disappear. I did not know what to do with this situation.

"Morning, Tina. Here, have some pancakes. The girls are enjoying their breakfast."

"Thanks, Mum, I will. Girls, come along and finish your breakfast."

"Mum, I need to buy the girls some clothes. Can you take me to a discount store?"

"Honey, do not worry about the girls. I woke up early and headed to Walmart where I bought some clothes and essentials."

I had not realized it before, but all the girls were wearing brand-new outfits.

I started crying in earnest. I could not believe how good my parents were. Even after the way I treated them, they still cared about me.

"Mama, why are you crying?" Rima asked. "Are you not happy you are here with Da and Ma? They are so good to us. See, they brought us new clothes. Mama, please stop crying. We are so happy to be here."

"I am okay, honey. I am crying because I am happy. I love your new clothes."

Feeling left out, Amira screamed, letting me know that she also needed my attention. My father set her on the floor. All three girls paraded up and down the kitchen, showing me their new clothes. They were so happy.

"Mum, Dad, I do not know how to thank you. I will never be able to repay you for all your kindness."

Facing My Actions

. . . .

"Tina, love, remember you are still our daughter. Jim, take the girls to wash their faces and then take them outside to play. Tina, it is time we talked. Your dad will take care of the kids."

The time had come for me to face the music.

My mum made us both cups of coffee, and we headed to the living room.

We sat on the couch, sipping our coffee. I was apprehensive because I knew this conversation was not going to be easy. I had done things that were not easily forgiven or forgotten. I knew no matter what my parents said, the hurt I inflicted on them was bubbling under their skin.

"Tina, I know you think we resent you, but we do not. We are still hurt by the injustices you have inflicted on us. I cannot lie to you and tell you all is forgotten. It has been a hard time for our family. We suffered from your actions. Our whole family was torn apart. As your parents, we love you no matter what, but to be honest we are still reeling from the way you treated us."

"Mum, I know."

"Tina, let me have my say. I know you are sorry and regret many things, but things are not going to be resolved over time. You need to be patient with us. We are going to support you no matter what, but it is going to take us some time for us to forget everything you have done."

Taking a deep breath, my mum continued.

"Both your brothers, David and Sam, refuse to have anything to do with you. They cannot easily forget the way you treated them.

They told us that they refuse to visit us as long as you are staying with us."

I started crying when I heard that. My own to brothers did not want anything to do with me. I could not blame them. I put my parents in a difficult position. My brothers refused to visit them if I was staying with them. That really hurt me.

"I am so sorry, Mum. I have ruined everything. I was so blinded by my so-called superior intellect that I destroyed all that was dear to me."

"We do not need you to be sorry, Tina. We need you to do something about this situation. You need to give your brothers time to forgive you. You cannot expect them to forget everything overnight. You might be sorry, but they do not care now. They think you got your just desserts."

"Mum, I will do anything to have my family back. I was a selfish, self-righteous idiot. I have missed my brothers so much."

"Tina, your actions started way before you met Jalal. You thought you could do no wrong. I know I did not want to bring it up, but all this need to be said. You called the police on us and nearly tore our family apart. We went through hell to get you kids back. You never listened to us. You nearly ruined our lives. We walked on eggshells to appease you. You brothers did everything to keep you happy. They bent backward to keep you happy. Your aunts, uncles, and cousins on both sides tired their best to befriend you. You were terrible to them. None of them want anything to do with you."

I should have expected this, but it still hurt. Thinking about my actions through the years, I was so ashamed of myself.

"David has recently gotten engaged and is getting married in six months' time. She is a wonderful young lady. Her name is Janet. She is active in her local Catholic church. She is an engineer. Sam is married and has twin sons. He named them Jim and David. He named them after his dad and brother. Your dad strutted for days after they were born. He married Jill, his high school sweetheart. You know Jill. She is a wonderful person. You were nasty to her when she came to visit us. She is a math teacher at the local high school. Sam adores her and the twins. They are adorable. Jill is such a sweetheart. She is there for us when we need her."

"Mum, I would like to make amends any way I can. I want to be part of their lives. I would love to meet my nephews."

"I am sorry, sweetheart, but it is not going to be easy. Sam does not want anything to do with you or your family. He does not want you anywhere near his family. He does not want you to adversely influence his kids. He is adamant about that. He also does not want to meet your daughter or stepdaughters. You do not exist as far as he is concerned."

Sobbing, I cried out, "Mum, what can I do to fix this?"

"At this time, nothing whatsoever. Give it time. Maybe he will look kindly on you in a few years. You have done enough damage as it is."

"What about David? Is he willing to see me?"

"David also refuses to have anything to do with you. Sam might eventually change his mind, but it is going to be much more difficult for David. This afternoon we are going to go to Sam's house for the twins' birthday. I am sorry you are not invited. We asked if we could bring Amira and the girls over, but Sam refused. He does not want anything related to you in his life. You do not know how hard this is for us. We refuse to interfere further. We do not want our family to fall apart because of this. Tina, you need to understand how we feel. Your brothers are not in the wrong—you are. I wish we had been firmer with you when growing up, and maybe all this would not have happened. Your father and I refuse to take sides. If we were forced to, you would not come out the winner. You are reaping what you sowed. We love you, but we refuse wipe the canvas clean."

"Mum, I am deeply hurt by all this, but I understand your position. I do not condone my brothers' actions. They are in the right, I know. It is just so difficult for me."

"It is good you understand. But we also talk about practicalities now. You need to plan. You have three little children to support. We will do our best to support you, but you need to get back on your feet. You had one more semester to graduate from nursing school. We have transferred all your credits to a local college near us. You are all set to start college in two weeks' time. We will support you until you graduate and find a job. Nurses are in high demand. You should not have any problems being hired."

"Mum, I do not know how to thank you."

"Thank me by working hard in school and getting a job. After that, you are on your own. After you graduate, we will help you get a place to live. We cannot have you staying with us forever. We usually host most holidays, and we want your brothers and their family over. They refuse to come over if you are staying with us. We will not forget you, but you need to understand that you are not a priority for us. We will do our best by you, but then you are on your own. You will be able to visit us, and we will help you as much as we can, but remember that you chose this path."

What my mother said was like arrows to my heart. I knew my family were hurt by me, but I did not expect all this. Maybe I was naive, but I thought they would accept back into their fold with open arms. I was paying the price of my actions.

"Mum, I understand how they feel, but my daughter in innocent of my actions. Could she at least be made to feel part of the family?"

"Tina, your brothers feel she might be tainted by your behavior. You are all sorry now, but what about later? They do not trust you a little bit. Do you blame them? If you reflected on your behavior through your adolescence until adulthood, you would understand where your brothers are coming from. You were a petulant spoiled brat.

"As for your girls, I am sorry if we cannot accept them fully into our family. I know they are innocent from all that happened, but they are a product of their environment. We will treat them well, make no mistake. As for Amira, we love her, but not like the twins. You made sure of that when you refused to let us see Amira when she was born. In your own words, you did not want our bad influence on her. Do you remember, Tina? What you said hurt us very much. We cannot forget all this."

My mother was crying hard as she made the last statement. It showed how deeply I had hurt her. I wish I could go back in time and

143

change all the wrong I had done to these wonderful people. After all the hurt and abuse I inflicted on them, they were still willing to help me. What a monster I was. I blamed Jalal for all my ills, but it was all my fault. How many lives had I ruined? How many people have I hurt with my thoughtlessness?

"Mum, I understand. Maybe one day you will forgive me. I realize it would not be easy, but I will do everything in my power for you and my brothers to accept me, even if it takes all my life."

"Just concentrate on healing and getting your life back together. I know you were physically and emotionally abused. I have gotten an appointment for you with a therapist to help you and the girls through this difficult time. You need professional help. This is non-negotiable for us. You and the girls are going to see her no matter what you say. Is that understood, Tina? I am not going to pander to your whims anymore. If you do not like it, tough luck. Here is the door, you can walk out anytime you want."

My mother was on a roll. I did not want to see a therapist, but I had no choice. Maybe my mother was right. I needed professional help to get me through this difficult time. I could not refuse anything my parents asked of me because I knew, deep down inside, they wanted the best for me. I looked outside the window and saw my dad playing with the girls. They were laughing and have a great time. I had never heard them laugh so much. This brought a smile to my face. These poor kids had been through so much. I needed to do all I could to keep them happy, healthy, and safe. As for Rima and Sahar, I needed to start the paperwork on adopting them. Jalal had already signed the document naming me as their guardian at the American consulate in Ibril. He wanted to make sure that they would be safe with me all the time. I did not know where he was, nor did I care. I knew he was going on a mission with the American forces back to liberate Mosul. I also knew that he would never make it out alive. I felt some regret for him, but I could not afford to dwell on it much. He had made me promise to take care of his daughters and raise them well. He also asked to expose them to his Islam. I had readily agreed to that but warned him that I would not force them to become Muslims.

"Tina, did you hear what I just said?"

"Sorry, Mum, I was just thinking about something. I will do as you say, Mum."

"Good. Your first appointment is this afternoon at three thirty. We are going to put a car at your disposal. Nothing fancy, but it is reliable. You still know how to drive, Tina?" my mother asked.

"Yes, Mum. I am a bit rusty, but I think I can manage."

"Good. Here is the address. Dad installed a navigation system for you in the car. I have brought you some clothes. They are in your room. We also opened a bank account for you. It is not much, but I think if you are frugal, you can manage. Here are the car keys, and this is your debit card. As for the therapist, the bill is taken care of. We were able to get you on Medicaid since you have no job."

"Mum, I do not know how to thank you, you really thought of everything."

"Do not thank us. Just get better and try to heal. We pray that in time your brothers will forgive you."

"I hope so, Mum, I hope so."

Going Shopping

"Okay, Tina, you still have time. Why don't we go to Walmart, and you can drive there? I want to make sure you still know how to handle the car. Your father will look after the kids until we come back."

"Are you sure, Mum? They would not tire him?"

"No, he loves kids. You should see him with the twins. He adores them. He talks to them every day. Jill is such a sweetheart. She makes sure to FaceTime us each day so that we can see the kids. They are adorable. They are the spitting image of your brother. We are so lucky to have such a beautiful daughter-in-law. She is like a daughter to us. As I was saying, your dad would not mind at all. Anyway, we had already discussed our plan with him before you came down this morning."

Hearing all this, I was sad. I was happy that my brother had a good wife who loved and treated my parents well, but on the other hand I was sad that I was not included in all this family love. I had no one to blame but myself. Even though I was to be blamed for all that was happening to me, I could not help but be hurt by the indifference of my brothers toward me. I knew my parents still cared for me, but deep down inside I felt their resentment. It was not overly obvious, but it was there in their body language and small hints they let pass. What did I expect? That they would accept me back with open arms and let bygones be bygones? I asked myself. I needed to face reality and realize it was going to take a long time for them to feel comfortable with me. I was a changed person. I had aged and matured a lot during this last horrific year in Mosul.

"Okay, Mum, let's go. I cannot thank you and Dad enough for all you have done for me."

146

"That is okay, my dear, we are still your parents. I also need to get some presents for the twins."

I smiled at that. "Mum, do you think I could send my nephews a gift for their birthday?"

My mum looked horrified. "I do not think it is a good idea. Your brother does not want anything to do with you. He will be upset if you send a gift, and you will put us in a very awkward position. We refuse to get involved between you and your brothers. We refuse to alienate our sons to appease you. Remember, Tina, even though you are our daughter, our sons are the ones that stood by us through all the years you made our lives a living hell. I am sorry."

I swallowed my tears. I did not want to show my mum how much her words hurt me.

"That is okay, Mum. I understand what you are saying. I know I should not expect a lot."

"Grab the car keys and let us head to the store. Your dad and I need to be at your brother's house at two thirty, and you need to be at your appointment at three thirty. I want to make sure you that you can handle the car."

We stepped outside and headed toward the car. It was 2005 black Honda Accord.

"Your father bought it for you when we realized you were coming back. It is in good shape and handles well. Having a car will help you be more independent."

With tears in my eyes, I hugged my mum. "Thank you, Mum. I do not deserve all this."

"Just get in the car and drive, Tina."

I got into the car and adjusted it accordingly. I slowly drove out of the driveway toward the shops. At first, I was a bit hesitant and nervous. I had not driven a car for at least two years. After around ten minutes, I got the hang of it. I felt liberated driving a car. When we arrived at Walmart, I found a parking spot and exited the car. I felt strange at first. I felt something was missing. Where was my hijab? I would get into trouble if someone saw me like this. I started to have a panic attack.

"Tina? What is wrong, my dear?" my mum's voice penetrated my panic.

"Mum, I am sorry. I felt that I had done something wrong. I panicked for a minute."

Mum looked at me in confusion.

"Mum, I was beaten a couple of times for showing an ankle in Mosul. I would have been killed if I walked dressed like this. I am sorry, it all came back to me. I panicked for a bit." Taking a deep breath, I continued, "I am okay now."

My mother looked shocked. He ran to me and hugged me tight.

"I am so sorry, my dear. You have been through a lot, I know. I do not know how to help me overcome all that you suffered. The only way I know how is to show you our support and love. I am more convinced than ever that you need professional help. You need to go to the therapist, my dear. Both you and the girls have been through hell. I am not equipped to help you."

"I know, Mum. Let head into the shop. I have not gone shopping in a proper store in more than two years."

I was still in daze but soldiered on. My mother realized that I was ill-equipped to deal with my situation. I could not burden her with all my problems. She had enough on her plate as it is. I did not want to add to her worries. The situation within our family did not help. My estrangement from my brothers was bothering her, but she did not want to get involved. She did not want to lose her sons because of me.

We went into the store, and for the first five minutes I was overwhelmed by everything. I was on edge if someone got close to me. I did not know what to do or were to shop for the things I needed. My mother had to guide me through it all. Finally, I was able to pick up some necessary clothes for myself and the girls. The girls were going to be so happy with their new clothes and toys. My mother, God bless her, insisted on paying for everything. She chose some books and two Busy Buggies for my nephews. We exited the store and went to the car and loaded all our purchases in the trunk. From there, my mother asked me to drive her to the local bakery to pick up the twins' birthday cake.

Returning Home from Shopping

By the time we returned home, I was both exhausted mentally and physically. The girls were excited by their new clothes and toys. Amira, still being young, did not care about anything except being fed, changed, cuddled, and put down for her nap. Sahar and Rima, on the other hand, could not contain their excitement. They insisted on trying on all their new clothes and showing them to Pa. They followed my father around like two lost puppets. I was surprised by this. Usually, the girls were terrified by strangers, especially men. But they seemed to love my dad. They could not finish a sentence without saying, "Pa did" that or "Pa said" that. I did not know how they communicated since their English was limited.

I was worried that they were bothering him. "Dad, I am sorry if the girls are being a nuisance."

Laughing, my father said, "Tina, these girls are sweethearts. They are easy to please. All they are asking for is a little attention."

"I know, Dad, but I know how much you dislike their father."

"Daughter, they are innocent of their father's crimes. Do not mistake me for the monster you married. I will never mistreat an innocent child. They are defenseless little kids that need all the love and attention you can give them. You have taken a huge responsibility. I hope you raise them well. I hope they do not make you go through what you made us go through." It was the first time my dad had mentioned my past behavior to me. I knew it was coming from a place of deep hurt and anguish.

"Dad, I cannot tell you how sorry I am."

"Tina, I do not want your apologies. I want you to live a better life and appreciate what you have. You were a holy terror. You destroyed many lives in your wake without much remorse. You have split this family apart with your selfish behavior. Do not do the same to these kids. I also blame both your mother and I for giving in to your blackmail. We will not do that anymore. Be warned. We love you and will always love you, but that does not mean we like you. It is going to take an exceptionally long time for me at least to trust you. You broke my heart, Tina. This is all I am going to say on this matter. Do not apologize again. Show me you are sorry by getting your life sorted."

"Yes, Dad."

Both the girls were exhausted, so I fed them lunch and put them for a nap. I wanted them to be ready to go to the therapist in the afternoon. I showered, relaxed for a while, and then got dressed. I woke the kids up, got them dressed, and shepherded them out the door.

A Year Had Passed

My therapist had been seeing me once a week for the last year. It had been a year since I got back from Iraq. Things were looking up for me. I graduated six months ago and secured a steady job as a registered nurse at our local hospital. I moved out of my parents' home into a three-bedroom apartment. The girls were attending the local school, and Amira was at day care. My parents helped me with looking after the girls, especially when I had to work night shifts. Life was looking up for me. My nightmares were slowly fading away.

Sahar and Rima were thriving. They felt secure and loved. I did my best to let them feel wanted and valued. They were going to school and enjoying it very much. I was amazed at how quickly they had picked up the English language. They refused to answer me in Arabic anymore. They had developed friendships. I tried taking them to the local mosque to teach them their faith. When they realized that I was not part of the congregation, they refused to stay. I told them their father wanted them to be brought up in his faith. They still threw a fit every time I tried dropping them off to religious school. Finally, I decided to hire a lady from the local mosque to come once a week to teach them the Muslim faith. I felt that they needed to learn their religion and heritage. Since I had renounced my Muslim faith, I could not in all conscience teach them. When they were older, it was up to them to decide what they wanted to believe in.

I tried to attend mass each Sunday. I had Amira baptized and decided to bring her up in the faith of my childhood. My parents were happy to witness the baptism of their granddaughter. They asked me if I wanted to baptize Rima and Sahar, and I told them

I cannot in all conscience do that. They needed to learn their dad's religion, and when they were older, they could decide what religion if any to follow. Both Mum and Dad applauded my decision. They felt it was not up to me to decide what path Rima and Sahar took. I could guide them but would not impose my views on them. I wanted my girls to grow up as independent, strong women. Life was good. I had a steady, well-paying job that I loved, parents who supported me, and daughters that I loved more than my life. The only black cloud on the horizon was my broken relationship with my brother.

I had recently received news that Jalal had lost his life during the liberation of Mosul. His brother Yousef, who was living in the Baghdad, got in touch with me and gave me the news. Jalal was fighting alongside the Iraqi Army. He was instrumental in the liberation of the city. I was sad for the man who he could have been.

I sat the Sahar and Rima down and gave them the news of their dad's passing. I was apprehensive at first. I did not know how they would react. To my shock they took it well.

"Sahar and Rima, I have some news to tell you."

"What is it, Mum?" Rima asked.

"Sweethearts, come sit next to me, please."

Both girls sat down next to me on the coach. One on each side. They looked scared.

"Mum, are we in trouble? Are you going to send us away? We promise to be good. Please do not send us away." They both started to cry. They were terrified I would turn my back on them. Poor babies, they had been through so much. I quickly tried to calm them.

"My dears, you are my daughters. You are not going anywhere. You are stuck with me. I love you so much. No one can separate us. Do you understand? Amira and I need you."

I felt them relax against me.

"Mum, we were scared you did not love us anymore."

"I will always love you. You are my daughters. You and Amira are my world."

The girls perked up after I reassured them of my love and commitment to them.

"Your Uncle Yousef, who lives in Baghdad, gave me the news of your dad's passing."

"What do you mean *pass away*, Mum?" asked Sahar.

"Your dad Jalal died and is with your grandmother in heaven."

"Are we going to see him again?"

"No, sweetie. I am sorry but we still have each other." Even though Jalal was their father, he was never close to them. He left their upbringing to their mum, who had abused them. He loved them in his own way, but he rarely showed it. They were not attached to his memory. I tried to keep his memory alive, thinking he would come back to see his kids, but it seemed it was not meant to be.

Both girls were upset. They cried a bit. They were enamored with the idea of having a father because many of their friends had one, but they never had one. He was a person who lived on the edge of their life. When we all lived together, I had observed that he never interacted with any of his children. He was busy with his work.

Then Sahar asked, "Mum, are you going to get married and bring us another dad?"

"Sahar, where did this question come from?" I was shocked by her question.

"I was just curious. My friend Amy has a dad."

"Sahar, you had a dad. He is not with you anymore, but he will always be your dad, sweetheart. He loved you both very much. Never forget that. He was not always present in your lives, but he loved you all very much. He sacrificed his life to keep you safe. Both you and Rima need to always remember that. When you are older, you will understand the sacrifices he did to keep you safe."

Jalal was not a good husband to me, but he was their father. He loved his girls very much. I knew that he redeemed himself at the end of his life, but I could not forgive him for the ordeal he put me through. I was not a naive fool to think that everything can be fixed with simple words and actions. I knew he sacrificed a lot for his family, but I never asked to be part of his plans to return to Mosul. I was not blameless; I had to take responsibility for my actions. Jalal never forced me to marry him or disown my family. I could have refused to travel to Mosul with him. But I could blame him for lying to me.

"Mum, can we go and play with Amira? She is all by herself in the room." Just like that, the conversation ended. The resilience of children.

Meeting with My Brothers

Dr. Patterson had insisted on a session that included all my family members. My parents were willing to join in some of the sessions, but my brothers were adamant on not being part of it. Finally, my parents convinced them to come. I was apprehensive about the meeting. I had missed my brothers so much. It was eating me from the inside out that they refused to have anything to do with me. Thanksgiving and Christmas had passed, and I spent them alone with the kids. Expect for Christmas morning where my parents came over and gave the girls their gifts, I was alone with my little girls. They left after a short time to spend Christmas Day at my brother's at Sam's house. I felt lonely and wanted to be part of the family again.

Were my brothers going to accept me back into the fold? Where they going to denounce me? I was terrified of this meeting. I knew that there was a lot of hurt and resentment on my brothers' part. Rightly so. I had worked through most of my problems. I knew I was not a victim but the oppressor, with my dealings with my family. I had hurt them deeply. I did not want to hurt them further. It was not my place to force them to accept me back into their lives.

I was sitting in my therapist's office with my heart in my throat. I was scared. I did not know what to expect. After what seemed like ages, David and Sam both entered the office accompanied by my therapist. They did not meet my eyes. They sat on chairs directly from me. My therapist, Dr. Sheila Patterson, cleared her throat and started speaking.

"David and Sam, I am glad you can finally meet with your sister today. There are many subjects we need to discuss here. I know that you did not want to come, but thank you for coming. Your sister, Tina, needs to talk to you and get things off her chest. She has been through a lot and needs your support if she wants to heal completely. Can you please share your feelings with us to try and bridge the relationship between you?"

Both my brothers looked at her as if she had lost her mind. David, always being the more vocal between them, could not keep quiet any longer.

"Dr. Patterson, I do not want you under any illusion here about our relationship with this woman. The only reason we are here is to appease our parents, especially our mother. She begged us to come. Because we honor and respect her, we came here to meet with her."

"David, I can see that it is not going to be an easy meeting, but I need you to have an open mind when your sister puts her cards on the table. She has been trying her best to heal the rift in your family. Your parents were amazing and participated in many sessions. I am asking you, please just listen, and then you can have your say."

"What can she say that will change our minds, Doctor? She destroyed our family and any filial ties between us. We begged and pleaded with her to listen to us, but do you know what she did?"

"I can see that this is not going to go as planned."

"David," I beseeched him, "I am really sorry for what I put this family through. Can you just give me a chance to make it up to you? I have been through so much." I was crying so hard, I could barely see in front of me. I was desperate for my brothers to listen to me. Maybe I was hoping for a miracle, but I wanted to be part of their lives. I was so lonely. I knew I should be grateful for all I had, but something was missing. My brothers were an integral part of my life. I wanted them there with me. I could not accept that they did not want anything to do with me. Was I asking for a lot? I did not know or care. My daughter needed to know her uncles. They were good and decent people, who would go out of their way to help anyone. They were always there for me in the past. They loved and protected me. I wanted that for my daughters.

"Stop with your crocodile tears, Tina, or whatever you call yourself. I am immune to your manipulations. If it were up to me,

I do not want to see you for the rest of my life. Have you not done enough? You are no victim. You hurt so many people in your life. You destroyed so many lives. Do you want to know what you did?"

"I think this is a good place to start, David," Dr. Patterson interjected. "Why don't you tell us what you think Tina did? Please, another important thing you need to remember, her name is Tina. This is important for you to remember."

All this time, Sam was quiet. He was observing the whole scene. I wondered what he was thinking but was afraid to find out. Sam had always been the less aggressive of the two.

"Where do I start, Doctor? I shall skip her selfish teenage behavior. She was a spoiled, entitled brat who thought the world revolved around her. What she wanted she got. She put our parents in a difficult position. They were terrified of losing their kids, so they needed to appease her whims. She never thanked them for all they did for us. In high school, she embarrassed us with her shenanigans. She never thought how her actions reflected on us. We put up with her and tolerated her actions to keep the peace in our family. She treated my fiancée, who was my girlfriend at the time, horribly. She made her the laughingstock of her class. She belittled her for her faith and beliefs. She thought it was funny and fun to make fun of a decent person. Jill put up with her behavior because she was my sister. If you meet Jill, you will understand what a sweet girl she is. She never harmed an ant in her life. Tina here was insanely jealous of her. She made her life a living hell throughout high school. Jill did not dare come over to our house, fearing Tina's reaction. Do you remember the names you called her, Tina? Or did you conveniently forget all that? You had your friends bully her."

As David was recalling all my bad behavior, I felt so ashamed of myself. I could not believe the way I behaved. It was all coming back to me. Jill was such a sweet girl. She never hurt a person. She never gossiped and was always nice to me and everyone around her. I was jealous of her relationship with my brother. My parents loved her, and I was not having her replace me in their affection. How stupid I was. I did not blame David for hating me. I hated myself.

David continued.

"When Tina went to university, we hoped she would change her attitude. She was our dear sister, and we were so proud of her. Our parents thought she would grow out of her viciousness. My parents always prayed that she would grow out of her rebellious stage. She would mature eventually. That was their excuse. Little did we know that she would become the worst bitch in creation. A nasty little piece of shit."

"David," Dr. Patterson interjected, "name-calling does not help anyone. Please remember that. We need to be civil here."

"She is right, David," Sam said. "Just tell Tina what you feel, but you do not need to call her names."

"You are absolutely right, Sam. I apologize, Dr. Patterson."

I realized that I had deeply offended and hurt these two wonderful men.

David was sorry for cursing me in front of Dr. Patterson, but he meant every word he said. I did not blame him. I was a horrible human being.

"While attending university, she imagined herself a social warrior intent on changing the world. I do not know if she told you her adventures at university. Instead of being grateful to our parents for sending her to college and paying for her tuition, she railed against them to anyone who would listen to her. My poor sister played the victim card to a tee. You see, to her my parents were bad people who treated her badly and hindered her mental and spiritual growth. Her venom also targeted anyone she deemed her adversary."

David was on a roll here. I knew he resented my behavior, but I did not understand how much until now. Seeing my behavior through his eyes, I was disgusted with myself. I really was a horrible person. How dare I ask for forgiveness from these people. They never harmed me. On the contrary, all they did was love and protect me. I, on the other hand, had betrayed them badly. It was inconceivable for me how much pain and suffering I had inflicted on them. I wanted to listen to everything they said. Every word they uttered was like a knife to my heart. It was a knife I had inflicted on myself. I realized that the person I hurt most of all with my actions was myself and my daughter through me.

"Tina, do you remember the Christian professors you nearly ruined?"

A vision came to my mind of a smug younger self. So proud of her accomplishments. I had harassed that poor professor until she had no choice but to resign from her position. "Yes, I remember her, David. I was stupid and hurt her."

"Sam, do you want to tell this part of the story? I think you should. Maybe then Tina can understand how far-reaching her actions were."

Looking at me with trepidation, Sam started his story.

"Professor Martilini is my wife's mother. She is one of the nicest people I know. She is devoted to her family and friends. She is a devoted Catholic. Her faith is her guiding principle. She lives her faith. She has never turned away any person in need. You took offense to her wearing a cross necklace and demanded she remove it. In your opinion, she was imposing her religious view on you. You harassed her and her loved ones until she was forced to leave her job. She got so many abusive mail and calls. The whole family was terrified of leaving their home. Her family suffered because of you. She had to hire a lawyer to get these trolls off her back. David took her case for free. He felt he owed her some reparation for the damage you inflicted on her.

"She was a wonderful professor. Her students loved her. They all vouched for her. A year later she was hired at another school. When I first met my wife, Janet, I was shocked to discover that my sister was the person who hurt her mother. It took me a long time to convince her of my true feelings. I cannot expect her to want to have anything to do with you. She does not want you around our family. You are toxic, Tina. You think you can do anything you want without any consequences. Do you think my wife should relive that upsetting time in her life? I love her with everything in me. I will put her and my two boys before anyone else. I am sorry, Tina, but you need to look at this from my point of view. My wife is a wonderful person. I bet she will forgive you and accept you into the fold, but I will not have her do that, especially at this time."

"Sam," I cried out, "I was an idiot. You do not know how much I regret my past actions. I have a daughter now, who I would die for. I also have two stepdaughters who I love very much. I can understand what you are saying."

"Let me ask you a question, Tina," Sam interrupted, "if your husband had not treated you badly and you suffered so much at his hands, would you realize the error of your past actions? That is one of the most important questions I have for you. Think on this question before answering."

"Sam, I do not know how to answer your question. I honestly do not know."

Dr. Patterson, who had kept out of our conversation so far, saw how upset I was and stepped in.

"I think this is enough for today. Tina, get your things together and go home. I need you to think on Sam's question, and we will meet next week to discuss it."

"Yes, Doctor. David, Sam, I hope we can talk again. Goodbye."

I left the room and headed home. My parents were at home babysitting the girls. My mind was in shambles. I was shaken by my first meeting with my brothers. At least they had opened to me. I felt there might be a chance we might have an amicable relationship, if not a close one. I was pondering the question Sam had posed. If Jalal had treated me better, would I still be the person I was? Would I still be the immature hypocrite I was back then? I suddenly realized I needed to forgive myself before asking others to forgive me. My sessions with Dr. Patterson were helping me. My parents were right in twisting my arm to go to her. She was a great doctor. I felt much better after each session.

"David, Sam, please take a seat. We need to discuss some issues relating to your sister's mental health."

Both David and Sam took a seat.

"Tina has suffered much during her time with her husband. She was abused very badly. I cannot delve into any particulars, but I can tell you that Tina has been through a lot. She needs your help to heal."

"Dr. Patterson, you cannot imagine what she has done to our family. We had just given you some highlights of her behavior."

"Maybe you can fill me in."

"This is going to be a long session."

David and Sam sat for around an hour talk to Dr. Patterson. I did not know much about what they said, but it seemed that Dr. Patterson had convinced them to come back for the following week. I thank God every day for Dr. Patterson. She helped me change my life. I know many say it is her job, but I think she is a miracle worker.

Another Family Session
with Dr. Patterson

The following week, I met with my two brothers at Dr. Patterson's office. Quite frankly, I was amazed that they were persuaded to meet with me again so quickly after our first meeting. I thought they were able to clear the air about their feeling, but was I in for a surprise. I am still—after many years have passed—shocked with what was about to be unraveled. I knew what a spoiled brat I was and how much damage my actions had caused, but today I was to discover how depraved I had been. How disturbing to one's mind was it to see events from another person's point of view.

"Hello, Tina," Dr. Patterson greeted me when I entered her office. "How are you doing today?"

"Hi, Dr. Patterson, I am doing well. It has been a busy week for me. The girls are doing well in school and happy with their lives. I am getting better. I am having less nightmares at night. I think I am getting better day by day."

"That is good to hear. Both your brothers will be here later, but first we need to discuss some issues. I need you to listen to me carefully. I met with them alone after you left last week. There are many issues that need to be resolved before any healing can take place. As your therapist, I need you to come to grips with your behavior in the past and deal with them. I need you to understand that we all make mistakes, but owning to our mistakes and getting on with our lives is what is important. You need to overcome your feelings of guilt and self-hatred for you to continue living a normal life. You cannot force anyone to forgive you or to forge a relationship with you. You need to accept whatever other people are willing to offer you. Keep that in mind when you listen to your brothers."

I nodded in agreement. What Dr. Patterson said made complete sense. It was not only up to me to build bridges between myself and my brothers. They had to be willing to give me a helping hand.

"Furthermore, Tina, there are certain dynamics in your upbringing that made you the way you are. I do not lay the blame of all your actions solely at your feet. From what I could surmise so far, you were spoiled rotten as a kid. You could do no wrong. Your family never reprimanded you for anything until it was too late. No one wanted to upset the princess in the family. This, in my opinion, contributed to your behavior later. You grew up with the idea that the world owed you everything. I will not say anything more on this topic until after our meeting with your brothers. Keep in mind, Tina, that David and Sam are very hurt. They were devastated that their beautiful and beloved sister would treat them in such a manner. They were your most ferocious defenders, and you betrayed them. It is difficult to overcome betrayal."

"I appreciate all that you are saying, Doctor, but I am also very hurt by all this. I want them to forgive me so much." I could not continue my sentence because my throat was choked up from tears. It hurt so much being rejected by my brothers. I did not appreciate how much until it happened to me. It has been a year since I came back home and still no thawing in our relationship. I had been patient and accepting, but this could not go on any further. They needed to understand how much I have suffered. I looked at Dr. Patterson.

"Don't you think my brothers are being a bit high-handed? I know I hurt many people with my past actions, but could they not let bygones be bygones? It is not fair how much they are dwelling on the past. I also have been hurt and abused. Why can't they just see things from a different angle?"

As soon as I said this, I realized how wrong I was. I was trying to deflect the blame and my problems on others. It was me who had broken our family ties. It was all my fault. I know I feel aggrieved now, but how did my family feel when I hurt them?

Dr. Patterson looked me in the eye and said, "Tina, think about what you just said. Do you even understand the gravity of your actions? I am not the one to pass judgment, but remember you are the person who wants to forge a relationship with your brothers. They were content ignoring your existence. Was it fair, what you just said? Do you think it is easy to build a relationship with you feeling this way? When your brothers join us for our session, I want you to listen and internalize everything they are going to say. I do not want you to become defensive. I just want you to listen. When they finish, you can chime in. Is that understood?"

"Yes, Doctor."

Listening to My Brothers

Finally, my brothers joined us for our session. Dr. Patterson greeted them and pointed to the seats opposite me.

"Hello, Sam and David. I hope you guys are doing well. I am glad you were able to join us today. Please take a seat."

They both nodded their greetings and sat down.

"Today, Tina is here to listen to everything you have to say. She is not going to remark on anything. I want her to look at events from your point of view. I only ask that you do not insult or demean her. I know you have bottled up your feelings for a long time, but we need to courteous."

"We understand, Doctor," Sam replied.

"Tina, you need to listen and not react to anything verbally. These things need to be said, and you need to hear them. Am I making myself clear?"

I nodded my head. I wanted to hear all what my brothers said. I knew it was not going to be pretty, but it had to be done. If a wound is not treated properly, it will fester. I did not want this deep wound between us to fester further.

"David, can you start please?"

"Where do you want me to start, Doctor."

"Anywhere you want, David. There is not a right or wrong way of doing this."

Taking a deep breath, David started his version of our relationship.

"Tina was our princess. We loved her so much. She could do no wrong in our eyes. Both Sam and I were overprotective of her. We spoiled her rotten. When she was younger, she adored us both and followed us both around. We did not mind it, because she was our baby sister. All her wants were catered to. Maybe that was where the problems started. We gave her everything she wanted, and that made her think she could do everything she wanted. Our parents were also smitten with their youngest child. They coddled her.

"As Tina got older, she became more demanding. Thinking everyone needed to acquiesce to her demands. Tina was a very smart kid. She knew she had my parents wrapped around her finger. What she wanted, she got. I do not think they grasped how much damage they were doing. When they realized their mistakes, it was too late to do anything about it.

"When Tina was a teenager, she wanted to go out and party every night. She had many boyfriends whom we did not approve of. They were mostly lazy, disrespectful, and into the party scene. We tried many times to talk to her about these scumbags, but she refused to listen to us. We had no right to interfere in her life. She knew what was best for her. She disregarded every single word we said to her. He family did not understand her. She was being suffocated by our concern. She wanted to live her life as she saw fit.

"When her boyfriend came to our home to take her with him to go and party, my parents for the first time in a long time refused to agree to her demands and blackmail. My parents turned her boyfriend away and told her to go to her room. She was to be grounded for the rest of the week. In my opinion it was about time they put their foot down. Little did we all know what a vindictive person out little princess was." David's voice started to shake with anger. To calm himself down, he took a deep breath and continued with his story.

"Tina went into her room, locked it, and destroyed every single piece of furniture there. She cried hard and inflicted some injuries on herself. Our parents tried to get her to open the door of her room, but she refused. She called the police and told them that she was being abused. When the police came and saw the bruises on her, she told them that her parents were abusing her. My parents were put in handcuffs and taken to the police precinct. Tina and I were taken into child protective custody. Sam was over eighteen, so he was left home. What happened after that was a nightmare. My parents were treated like criminals, and the family was torn apart. I was terrified that I would not see my family again. After a long time, my parents were finally able to reunite with us. From that day on, Tina got everything she wanted. She walked all over us. I left for college a year after that, but my parents were never the same after that. They still loved their little princess but were scared she might call the police on them. This was a turning point in our family dynamics. I felt resentment toward Tina. Tina got away with all her bad behavior. She partied to her heart's content. She dated the worst possible guys. They were good for nothing. She brought them home and forced my parents to accept them. Thank God I was not there to see all this. My fiancée, who was is a couple years younger than me, felt the brunt of Tina's vindictiveness. At first, I did not believe her and always made excuses for Tina's behavior, but in the end, I had to face reality. My sister was not a pleasant person, but she was still my little sister, and I felt compelled to protect her."

David was so affected by the recalling of the story that he could not continue. I was shocked by how emotional David was. I did not think of the effect all this had on David. My guilt increased with each retelling of my behavior. I had no excuse to give. I was a wild child. I dated many bad guys. I partied so hard. My parents were upset and hurt, but I did not believe that my brother also cared.

David looked me in the eye. "Tina embarrassed us during her high school years. Everyone was talking about my whore of a sister who dated any boy she took a fancy to. She even fought other girls she thought were infringing on her territory. I was so ashamed of her actions. Her reputation was in tatters. Everyone gossiped about her. My parents were hurt deeply."

Seeing my behavior through David's eyes, I did not feel particularly good about myself. I know I was a brat, but I never thought about how it would feel for an older brother to feel about his sister's dating behavior. I always assumed that they did not care how many guys I was dating. I was having fun. What did it matter what I did? It was a bit disconcerting to realize that my brothers were chauvinists.

The thought had not entered my mind when David blew this theory out of the water.

"How would Tina have felt if Sam and I dated indiscriminately? Would she have been fine with it? What if we had bought all sorts of girls to meet our parents and younger sister. What if these girls were disrespectful and abusive toward our family? Would that be all right with everyone?"

He looked straight at me when he asked the question. He could see how shocked I was by his question.

"I know how you think, Tina. You were going to argue about the equality of the sexes and how hypocritical I am. We wanted you to date a decent person. The guys you bought home were a disgrace. They showed no respect toward you or our parents, but it was all right with you. You did not care how your parents suffered. What you wanted, you got. What happened is a consequence of your actions. You cannot go through life doing what you want, without facing any consequences."

That really got to me. I did not recall that my behavior was that bad. I remember when I was still in Mosul overhearing the conversation between Jalal and Samira. They had said the same thing. It was evident that I could not lay all the blame on Jalal and his family on the situation I was in. My family did not abandon me. I abandoned them with my sheer stubbornness and selfishness. I could not blame Sam and David with their refusal to have anything to do with me. Every time I listen to events from their point of view, I hated myself. Before making amends to my family, I needed to forgive myself.

"Tina," Sam interjected, "do you remember the last time you saw us before you got married and moved overseas?"

How could I forget that day? It was seared in my brain. I acted like a jerk. Demeaning and insulting my brothers. I called them all kinds of names. They begged me to listen to them, to no avail. I threatened them with the police and told them I did not want anything to do with them. I treated them like my worst enemies. I did not care how my words and actions hurt them. I could not contain myself anymore. Even though Dr. Patterson had told me to just listen to Sam and David, I had to say something.

"David, Sam, you do not know how sorry I am for the way I acted that day. I am so ashamed for the way I treated you. I behaved like a jerk. Please listen to me. I was blinded by my love for Jalal and wanted to do everything in my power to please him."

"Tina, please stop. Do not put all the blame on your husband. You are not blameless in all of this. No one put a gun to your head and told you to act the way you did. I do not care how much you thought you were in love with someone. This does not excuse your actions. You threw us in jail, Tina. You called the police on us and accused us of threatening your life."

"What are you saying, Sam? I never called the police on you." I was shocked by Sam's accusation. I had not called the police on my brothers. I had threatened them with the police, thinking to scare them away, but would have never gone through with it. This was all news to me. What was going on here? I needed to get to the bottom of this.

"Tina, do not insult our intelligence. It is not the first time you have called the police on your family. Do you think we will believe you?"

This was crazy. I do not know why they would think that. I was guilty of many things, but this was something that cannot be laid on my door.

"Listen to me, both of you, I never called the police on you. I know I threatened you with the police, but that was it." I was not going to let them accuse me of this heinous act. I was on the brink of losing my temper. I had played the victim for a long time. This had to stop. I know what I did was wrong, but I would not be blamed for things I had no hand in.

Dr. Patterson, seeing me getting angry, tried to defuse the situation.

"Let us not get into this at this moment. Please, Tina, you need to listen to your brothers. We need to find out what really happened. David, can you take over and tell us what happened."

"Yes, Doctor. It was an awfully bad time in our lives. It is exceedingly difficult for me to think about it."

"I understand, David," Dr. Patterson said, "but we need to see it from your point of view."

"Tina was in her senior year of college. She had one semester to graduate as a registered nurse. We were all so proud of her. She was still belligerent and spoiled, but she was our beloved little sister. I had just graduated from law school the year before and was working at a law firm. Sam graduated from engineering school and had landed a great job. Suddenly, she cut all contact with us and our parents. Both Mum and Dad tried to talk to her many times, but she refused to talk to them. She called them all sorts of names and even threatened them if they called her. She told everyone that she had found true meaning in Islam. She had converted to Islam and wanted nothing to do with us. She did not tell us that she had dropped out of college. She used the money my parents had put aside for her tuition and living expenses to support her husband and his family. The money my parents worked so hard to save toward her education. Not only did she lie to my parents, but she also stole their money."

Dr. Patterson could not hide the shock on her face when hearing this latest tidbit. I knew she needed to stay impartial in this discussion, but how could she after hearing what I did? She quickly rearranged her features to a more neutral expression. I did not blame her. What I did was awful.

"Tina, is what your brother said true?"

"Yes, it is, and I have no excuse for what I did. I cannot defend my actions. I did take my parents' hard-earned money and spend it on Jalal and his family."

I started sobbing at this point. I could not control myself. Even after I stole my parents' money, they still supported me after I came back from Iraq. They paid for my last semester at college and helped me with the girls. They even bought me a car. I could not but be overwhelmed by their love and generosity. This was true love. Love was not destructive and blind.

"Please forgive me, but…" I could not continue with my sentiment. What could I say to these two men who had been there for me all my life? I had used their love for me to hurt and abuse them.

Dr. Patterson, seeing my reaction to all this, put a stop to our session.

"Sam, David, I think we need to take a break. Can you come next week? I think Tina is overwhelmed by all this."

Both my brothers looked at me and scoffed. They both left without saying a word, but I felt they did not believe I was upset. They thought I was acting to get their sympathy. They did not trust me to have any finer qualities. My heart was breaking. Who could blame them? Now I know how they felt when I disregarded their love and feeling for them. I threw their love and regard back in their faces. I understand how reluctant they were to give me the benefit of the doubt.

Be Honest with Me

"Tina, Tina..." Dr. Patterson was trying to get my attention. I was so deep in thought that I forget about her presence.

"Sorry, Doctor, I was deep in thought."

"Yes, I can see that. Can you come back to the present, please?"

"Yes."

"It seems there are many issues that you have kept from me. If you want to move forward with your therapy, you need to be honest with me. You have kept things from me. I was blindsided when David told me about the tuition money. I am not here to judge anyone, but you needed to be honest with me. Your brothers were deeply hurt by the way you used your parents' hard-earned money to support your husband and his family."

"Doctor, I am so ashamed of my actions. I do not know why I kept it to myself. My brothers are rightfully furious with me. It seems I have been nothing but a burden to all of them."

My sobbing had increased by that point. I could not talk.

"Calm down, Tina. I know you are upset, but how do you think your family feels? It is imperative that you realize there is no magic pill that can solve everything. You need to work hard to earn their trust again. It might take years, it might never happen, but at least you are trying. Remember one positive aspect in all this. You parents did not turn their backs on you. They helped you and supported you after you returned into the fold. They can also influence your brothers. The love and respect your brothers have to your parents is the reason they are here. Your parents' love for you will be your saving grace."

Listening to her, I felt hopeful. Maybe I was grasping at straws, but I needed to keep my moral high. I realized that I needed to be honest with Dr. Patterson. I needed to tell her everything. Even my most embarrassing actions. It was not going to be easy, but I needed to do it.

"Dr. Patterson—" I said.

"You know what, Tina," she interrupted, "I think it is time you started to call me Sheila."

"Sheila then. I am going to tell you everything from a to z."

"Good. Why don't we start now?"

"I left many things out, but before we start, I need to let you know that I never called the police on my brothers after our meeting. I have a suspicion who did. You see Khadija, Jalal's first wife, followed me to our meeting. Jalal did not trust me alone, so it seems he sent her to spy on me and make sure I stayed the course. You know how much she abhorred me. She wanted to hurt me any way she could. She was deranged, and Jalal was blind to reason. I think after I returned form the meeting, she said something to Jalal, and he called the police on them. They wanted me to make sure I was under their control. That is one crime they can lay on me."

"I believe you, Tina. Please continue."

"You know, Sheila, I was so blinded by my love for Jalal that I could not fathom anyone standing in my path. I wanted to eliminate all obstacles in my path. It is disgraceful how I behaved."

"Tina, do you think that Jalal was the root of all your problems? Look back at your behavior since high school. The way you behaved and the way you treated the people around you. You felt that the world owed you everything. You trampled on everyone in your path to get what you wanted. In Jalal's case, you saw him and wanted him. You did not care who you hurt if you got him. You changed your life, converted to his religion, and lived by his edicts because you wanted him. Jalal did not force you to do all that. Think, Tina, of your track record."

"Sheila, Jalal and his aunt Samira said the same thing. They said that I was as much to blame for the situation I found myself in. I can see their point of view. Jalal was possessively jealous of anyone who got close to me. He knew of my dating history and assumed that I would easily fall for any guy who talked to me. He saw my behavior with my parents as a sign that I cannot be trusted. It is ironic how he pushed me to cut all ties with my family, but when I did what he told me to do, he resented me more. In his culture, parents are respected and esteemed."

"Do you see a pattern here, Tina?"

"Yes, I can see a pattern. I went after what I wanted without thought of the consequences. I wanted to party and date whoever I wanted, so I called the police on my parents to force them to back down. I wanted to make an example of Professor Martilini for being a Christian, so I harassed her and nearly ruined her life. I wanted Jalal, so I did everything in my power to get him, even alienating myself from my family and friends."

It scared me how dedicated I was to achieving my goal. Even if these goals were destructive to others or to oneself. I had tunnel vision where my ideals were concerned. I felt that a lot of what happened to me in Mosul was my fault. Jalal being from a different background did not see me as a virtuous woman. He wanted me, and the only way to have me was through marriage. In his belief, he needed to marry someone to have a physical relationship with them. I thought he respected and esteemed me when he said we needed to wait until we get married to have a physical relationship. In my ignorance, I thought I was his one and only. I even thought my experience would be a benefit for both of us. I was going to teach him the joys of the flesh. It was a very new way of looking at things. I did not see the abuse because in my mind I did not want them to be there. When Jalal and his family called me a whore, they meant it. They considered my relationships with other men as a taboo. Jalal was demeaning himself by marrying me. In their opinion, he could have just kept me as his concubine. In their belief, he could sleep with a woman who was not of the faith. I knew that and was amazed he wanted to wed me. It does boggle the mind, but at the same time it made perfect sense.

"I am glad you were able to understand. Dedication is not a bad thing, but you need to focus on achieving positive outcomes without hurting others. You are not entitled to everything you want. There are always two sides of a coin. Your way of thinking is not always the best one. Other people have different points of view. You need to respect that." Sheila stopped and took a deep breath. I could see that my session with her was draining. There were many issues to discuss.

"The world does not revolve around you, Tina. You need to realize how fortunate you are. I know how much you suffered during your marriage. It could have broken a lesser person, but you survived. Keep something important in mind—you would not have suffered at all if you were a bit flexible. If you had listened to your loved ones. You threw yourself in a relationship without counting the consequence. You knew what was best for you. Everyone was evil, and you were the savior of the world. You paid a heavy price for your actions. I am sorry to be tough on you, but you need to hear it. Your hackles went up when David and Sam were critical of your dating history. Without even knowing what they wanted to convey with their criticism, you automatically assumed they did not want you to date because you were a girl. Do you agree with me, Tina?"

"I know, Sheila, you are right. I thought they were angry because I was dating. I did not realize they were upset at the caliber of boys I was dating. They were horrible guys. They drank, smoked, and partied. I thought they were so cool. I was passed around from one boy to the next. I became one of the popular girls because I gave them what they wanted."

"Tina, I am not criticizing you or telling you what you did was wrong. I am just saying you need to look at everything they say with an open mind. You cannot take issue with what they are saying. Their feelings have been bottled over the years. It is the first time they are able to open up about their own feelings."

"Sheila, I did many things that are indefensible. I did use my parents' money to support Jalal and his family. I did call the police on my parents when I was a teenager. I reveled in the fact I had this control over them. I blackmailed them into doing whatever I wanted. I treated my professor very badly. I also hurt and abused Janet, David's fiancée. I was such a hateful person. I ruined many lives. I could have gone through my whole life ignorant of the hurt I caused if it were not for the consequence of my actions. That is the part that scares me most, Sheila. I get nightmares thinking about it. If I had not landed in this mess, would I have woken up to what I have done?"

"Tina, it is not easy admitting you have wronged so many people. You yourself needed to realize it. You would not have accepted anyone telling you of the error of your ways."

Sheila was on a roll. I could see that she wanted to continue talking to me, but she stopped suddenly.

"You know what, Tina, you look exhausted. You have been working overtime at the hospital and taking care of the girls. You need to go home and relax. We can continue our session next week. Both David and Sam have promised to attend it."

I was emotionally and physically drained. I had the weekend off, and I planned to spend it relaxing with the girls. I planned to take them to the park and then maybe out to lunch. They were such good and happy girls. They rarely gave me a hard time. I knew that my parents were invited to my brother David's new house. He had planned a housewarming party for the whole family. My mother had mentioned it in passing. I of course was not invited. David and Janet, his fiancée, did not want me in their home. Even though I understood why they excluded me, it still hurt.

I got up from my seat, thanked Sheila, and left for my parents' home. My parents were babysitting my girls today. My girls adored my parents. My dad was their hero. They followed him around. I smiled, thinking about how much love they were receiving from my parents. It was heartening to realize how fortunate I was to have such loving and caring individuals in my life.

A Pleasant Surprise

··

When I entered my parents' house, Rima and Sahar barreled toward me, with Amira trotting after them.

"Mum! Mum!" they screamed. "Guess what?"

They were both talking at the same time, that I did not understand what they were saying. All I could make out was *Uncle David* and *brother*.

"Calm down, girls, you seem overly excited. Go get ready, and we can go home."

"But, Mum," they whined, "we want to stay here with Pa and Ma and have dinner."

"Girls, why don't you go to the next room and watch television with Pa?"

They ran out of the hallway so fast, I could barely make a protest. Even Amira ran after them on her tiny feet.

"Mum, what is going on?"

"Tina, I promised the girls they can have dinner with us. I am making burgers and fries, their favorite meal."

"No, Mum, that is not what I meant. How do they know about Uncle David?"

"Well, Tina, David stopped by to pick up a dish I made for tomorrow. He met the girls. At first, he was shocked to see them here, but they won him over. They are such good girls, easy to please. Amira attached herself to him and would not let go. It was funny how enamored she was of him. Rima and Sahar were hesitant at first but decided he must be a good guy, because they also clambered all over him. They made him sit on the couch and sat on his lap, asking him multiple questions. Let me tell you, David was bewildered and did not know what to do."

I started crying at this point. David did not reject my daughters. I had started thinking of Sahar and Rima as my daughters a long time ago. They were daughters of my heart, if not my body. The adoption papers had gone through, and they now belonged to me. I loved as much as I loved Amira. The girls were my world, and I was protective of them.

"Tina, sweetie, what did you expect David to do? Reject the girls? They are innocent of any wrongdoing. I know I said we cannot accept them into our family, but I was wrong. Your dad and I have become attached to them. They have sneaked into our hearts without even trying. Even your brothers acknowledge that. We love all three girls equally. They are starved for love."

"I know, Mum, but Sahar and Rima are not related to him."

"Tina, Sahar and Rima are innocent little girls. We never resented them. What we resented and were offended by was your behavior. We do not even resent Jalal and his family. They grew up in a different society and religion. Jalal and his family did what they saw fit for themselves and their family. We understand that. We do not judge them. What we were hurt most by was how you rejected all your values and blindly followed Jalal. You might not want to hear what I am saying, but it needs to be said. We were always good to you. We treated you like a princess, but you turned your back on us. This is something that we can never forget. It is like a scare on our heart."

My mother was silent for a moment, and taking a deep breath, she tried explaining how she felt by my abandonment of the family.

"We gave you everything you wanted, but it was never enough. We protected you and loved you. You threw all that in our faces. We even came to grips with you when you converted to Islam and marrying Jalal, but it was still not enough for you. You called us all kinds of names. You accused us of horrendous crimes, shutting us out of your life completely. You called us infidels, scum of the earth. You even threatened to call the police on us and file a restraining order. How much more abuse can someone take?"

"Mum, don't you think I have suffered enough rejection to last me a lifetime? I understand what I did, but I just need a break."

"Oh, sweetie, what do you think we have been doing, if not giving you a break? We have supported you and helped you get on your feet. Both David and Sam agreed to go to your therapy sessions. They even contributed financially toward your last term at college and buying you a car. It is not easy for any of us to forget what you did. We have suffered greatly because of your actions. Since you were a teenager, you rebelled against us. We almost lost our children. Jobs and home because of your actions. Do not play the victim with me, Tina. I am your mum, and I know you. I believe that you are contrite, but you need to give us all time to overcome the abuse we endured at your hands."

I was shocked by this piece of news. I had never in a million years dreamed that my brothers were helping me out financially. After all I have subjected them to, they still went out of their way to help me.

"Mum, did you ask them to help me?"

"No, Tina, we did not. Both David and Sam knew that supporting you would put a strain on our finances, so they offered to help. At first your dad and I refused their contributions, but they insisted. They claimed they did not want us to struggle financially. I am grateful that God gave me such good children. They have been a great help though all our lives. They were there for us when your dad had his stroke after you left the country. Thank God it was a mild stroke, and your dad got through it. Both your brothers and their significant others never left our sides. Jill and Janet were amazing. I love them as much as I love my sons."

This was news for me. I was never told that dad had a stroke. He seemed fine to me.

"Mum, you never told me had a stroke. When did this happen? Why was I never told?"

"There are many things that you do not know about. When you refused to see us after you gave birth to your daughter, your dad took it hard. He stopped taking care of himself and was drinking and smoking heavily. As a result, he had a mild heart attack. It was a wake-up call. He stopped drinking and smoking and got into shape. It was a difficult time for us. We were worried sick for your dad's health and fretted for not knowing about what happened to you. We had lost our daughter and were afraid of losing your dad."

I hated that I was the cause of my father's illness. What amazed me most is my parents' love and support of me even after all the trouble I have caused.

"Mum. Do you know how much I love you? I have caused much misery in this household, yet you still support and love me. I hurt my brothers badly, but they still financially supported me without being asked. I am so lucky. Mum, I will never be able to repay you for all you did for me. I do not deserve you."

I was so honored to be part of this family. After all my destructive behavior, I did not expect such kindness.

"Sweetie, yes, you behaved very badly, and your behavior caused much grief. But we need to get over it. Even your brothers and their significant others are realizing they need to patch up their relationship with you. You need to give them time to come to terms with all that has happened. Do not expect miracles, but I believe things will get better eventually."

"I hope so, Mum. I am praying every day that they will forgive me. I want them in my life. I pray that both Janet and Jill accept me as their sister-in-law. I have wronged them both."

"David and Jill have decided on a wedding date. They have already booked the church and the venue. I am so excited for my son's wedding. Jill has always been here with us in good and bad days. She was the daughter I wished I had. She stood by us when your dad had his heart attack. She is a wonderful girl. I pray that they include you in their wedding."

I felt hurt and ashamed when I heard my mum's praise of Jill. Hurt because I was never the daughter she was proud to call her own. Ashamed because my actions have branded me a pariah of the family. I was never there for my parents in their time of need. I followed my wants and desires, abandoning them at the worst possible time in my life. I wanted to be invited to my brother's wedding. I wanted to celebrate this important milestone in his life. It hurt so much to be on the outside looking in. I wanted my girls to feel part of this loving family, growing up with their cousins. Was it too much to ask for? I have come to grips with my actions. I have forgiven myself and looked forward to a new life. I knew I could not change the past. All I can do is live a better life. All I was seeking was acceptance into the fold. God help me, but I will never rest until I achieved my goal. I needed to be patient, but in the end, I believe things will improve. In the meantime, I needed to focus on helping my girls and building bridges with my loved ones. My little girls would love to be part of the wedding. I felt empty inside. I hoped David and Jill would be able to forgive me and ask me to attend the wedding.

"Mum, thanks for looking after the girls. I need to take them home. They have school tomorrow. They need to get to bed soon."

"They already had their dinner. I have some for you to take home."

I gathered my girls and headed home. On the way back home, the girls could not stop taking about David. They thought he was a great guy. Amira even chimed in the conversation.

"Mama, when can I play with Unca Dave?"

"Oh, sweetie, Uncle David is a busy man. I do not know when he will be available. I will ask Grandma, okay?"

"Okay, Mama. Love Grandma, Papa, and Unca David. Love you, Mama. Love Rim and Saha."

My daughter was adorable. I loved her so much. Rima and Sahar where extremely protective of her. She was spoiled rotten by them. I did not want her to grow up like me—entitled and a spoiled brat. I made sure she knew her boundaries and was punished when she overstepped them. I did not want her to think she could do whatever she wanted. She had just turned two. She was into everything. She was also loving and friendly.

"We love you too, little sister," chimed Rima.

These were my girls, the center of my world. Who would have thought that I would come to love Sahar and Rima this much? I thanked God every single day for them. They have thrown away the shackles that bonded them from birth. All they knew for the first years of their lives was an abusive mother and an absent father. They were berated, beaten, and belittled. They could do nothing right in their mum's eyes. They were the punching bag for their nasty older brother. Despite all this adversity, they were loving and sensitive young girls. They were appreciative of any kindness shown toward them. They adored my parents and thought the world of them.

When we got home, I put my daughters to bed and sat down to have dinner. I kept thinking of David and his fiancée, Jill. Was there a chance I could mend fences with them? Should I initiate any communication with Jill? Would she be open to talking to me? I did not know what to do at this point. I was desperate. I did not want to make David angry at me and destroy the fragile channels of communication we had. I was in a dilemma. I thought hard about it and decided to talk with Sheila about it.

Counseling

Here I am again waiting for David and Sam to join us in my session. I took the opportunity to talk to her about how to approach David and his fiancée, Jill.

"Sheila, I want to ask you a question, but I am afraid what you might say."

"What is it, Tina? You need to tell me what is on your mind. For you to heal, you need to be honest with me. Please tell me what is going on."

"My brother David is getting married in six months' time. My parents love his fiancée, Jill. They are so excited. I feel ostracized by my family. My brother has no intention of including me and my girls in his wedding celebration. I was wondering, should I contact Jill, his fiancée, and try to mend my bridges with her? Do you think it is a good idea to try and reach my brother through her?"

"Tina, think carefully about all this. Do you remember how badly you treated Jill when you were in high school? You were not a nice person to her. Do you think she can overlook the abuse you dished out? She also saw how abusive you were to the man she loved."

"I know all that, but I feel lonely. I want to be part of their lives. I want to attend their wedding. I want my girls to grow up knowing them. Rima and Sahar met David the other day. They were at my parents' when he dropped by. The girls fell in love with him. They attached themselves to him and would not let go. By the time I got there to pick them up, he was gone. My mum told me about how much they were mesmerized by him. They could not stop talking about him."

"Hold on, Tina. There are a couple things here that we need to address. First, you talk about your wants, not what your brother wants. You want to attend the wedding, so you want to find a way to be there. Do you agree with me?"

"What do you mean, Sheila? I do not understand what you are getting at."

"Did you think about Jill and using her to get your brother to accept you back into the fold? Think about it. Did you consider how this might have affected Jill's relationship with your brother? Tina, you need to think carefully before acting. The world does not revolve around your wants and needs. You need to be patient. It is up to your brother when he will accept you back into his life."

"But I do not mean it to be this way."

"Tina, think of others before you come up with your plans. I am not denying that you are frustrated and want things to happen, but you need to be patient. You cannot use underhanded ways to get what you want."

"I do not want to see to that. I thought it was a good idea."

"Like you thought it was a good idea to push away your family."

I teared up with hearing her comment. She was right, but did she have to be so brutal. Reminding me of my lowest point in my life."

"It seems, Tina, you do not to be reminded of how your actions affected your family."

"It was a low blow, Sheila. Did you have to remind me of my despicable actions? I am trying my best to get over my actions. I am bending backward to make up for my actions."

"Tina, you need to understand how things work. You need to remember what you did, so as not to repeat them. I am not trying to hurt you but reiterate my point. Both your brothers need time to heal. You are not the only one who suffered in this ordeal. You are the aggressor as much as a victim. Your family never hurt you. They suffered because of you. Yet they still supported you when you needed them most. Even your brothers helped you when you came back. They helped you get on your feet."

"It still hurts, Sheila. What you said still hurts. I know you are right, but I am human after all. Words hurt."

"How do you think Sam and David felt when you turned your back on them? You hurt them badly, and yet you still think it is not okay for me to tell you so. Think hard, Tina. I know you need to forgive yourself for your actions, but at the same time you cannot repeat them."

"It is just difficult for me to internalize all that you are saying. I cannot but feel hurt by all that is going on. I feel as if I am on the outside looking in. It hurts because my girls are being left out. They might not feel it at this time, but when they get older, they are going to start questioning me, why we are always not invited to family get-togethers. I understand my family's stance, but I also want to protect my girls. I do not want them to feel unwanted. They are innocent of all my sins. Why should they pay the price of my actions? This is what is the most hurtful aspect of it."

"I know where you are coming from, Tina. I understand your concerns. Maybe you should bring this situation up to your brothers."

"Do you think they will try and accommodate my girls in their lives?"

"Tina, you cannot use the girls to get what you want. They might see right through you if you do that. You need to approach this a subtle manner. Sam and David would be here soon, so we need to focus on unsolved issues before attempting to bring in any other topic. Is that understood? Do not sever the fragile ties we have built."

"Okay."

I understood what she said and realized she was right. I needed to be patient with my family. I cannot impose myself on them after all the wrongs I have committed. I needed to show them I was trustworthy before attempting to insert myself into their lives. The wound was still raw. It needed to heal before anything further could happen.

David and Sam arrived promptly at the office. They both looked grim and apprehensive. Today was the day that everything was going to be brought up in the open. Sheila had booked the whole afternoon for this session. I was also scared. I did not know what they were going to say or do.

"Hi, David and Sam. I hope you had a good week. Please take a seat so that we can begin. Today you are going to lay all your cards on the table. I want to hear everything you have to say."

Both nodded and took the seats opposite me.

"David, please, can you begin?"

"Yes, I am going to talk about the day that both Sam and I both decided to disown Tina."

"Please go ahead, David. Both Tina and I both want to understand what happened that day."

"We phoned Tina, begging her to meet us and discuss our relationship with her. We were worried about her. We were not comfortable with her life choices and wanted to warn her. We also wanted to tell her how much we loved her and would support her no matter what she decided. We were not expecting her vicious and unwarranted actions. I can still remember how nasty she was toward us. She railed against us and called us all sorts of names. In her eyes we were her enemy, below her notice. It seems she had found a new family and did not want anything to do with our toxic presence. She stormed away in a huff. We were hurt and upset but decided it would all blow away, and she would realize how much we loved her. Little did we realize what a nasty and vindictive person she was."

"What happened, David, to make you and Sam turn your backs on her?" Shelia prodded.

"We did not turn our backs on her, Dr. Patterson. What she did to us was unforgivable." Sam interjected in a forceful voice. "Do you want to know what Tina did? I shall tell you. She nearly destroyed our lives. I thank God each day that David was a lawyer and had connections. He was able to get us out of the mess she got us in. Just thinking about it makes my blood boil. I cannot imagine Tina would do a horrible, vindictive deed."

I was shocked by what Sam was saying. What did I do to them that nearly destroyed their lives? I just left in a huff. Granted I was rude, vicious, and abrupt, but I did not do anything else.

Taking a deep breath, Sam continued with relating the events that made me a pariah in their eyes.

"After Tina left in a huff, we sat down trying to discuss our dilemma. We were hurt and upset but thought she will eventually come around. Suddenly two police officers entered the coffee shop. They came toward us and explained that they needed to take us into custody. We both thought it was a joke. We asked the officer what the problem was, and he claimed that two women have complained that we were harassing them. They claimed we targeted them specifically because they were wearing a veil and were of the Muslim faith."

Turing to me, Sam said, "Who could it be other than you, my dear? They even said the complaint was in your name and another woman named Khadija."

I was dumbfounded by his accusation. I had not called the police on them. Before I could defend myself, David took over from Sam.

"It seems our dear sister had called the police on us, citing Islamophobia as the reason. She claimed we followed her around, tried to rip the veil from her head. Spewing abuse at her. She also claimed we threatened to do her bodily harm if she did not renounce her new faith. The claim also stated that we have been targeting her for a while. She was terrified for her life and the life of her husband and his family. Yes, our dear sister falsely accused us of these heinous crimes."

David was too upset to continue, so Sam took over.

"They handcuffed us and took us to the police station. On the way there, David told me to keep quiet and not say a word. When we got to the station, David asked to speak with his lawyer. He called his law firm and asked one of his colleagues to come down and help us out. We waited for an hour until our lawyer came down to the station. He met with us, and David told him all that had happened. The lawyer was shocked by these accusations. He had been friends with David for a long time. He knew that what he was accused of was bullshit. He also knew that we loved our sister and would never do such a thing to her. He posted our bail, and we went home."

David then looked me straight in the eye and said, "Do you know it took us months to clear our name? We had to appear in court multiple times before we could prove our innocence. Both of us nearly lost our jobs. Thankfully, we had many friends and colleagues who were willing to vouch for us. We were also lucky that the evidence that you fabricated was thrown out. It took us nearly a year to clear our names. Do you think we should overlook this event, forgive, and forget? Every time I think of what you did, I resent you more. What more damage do you want to do, Tina? Have you not hurt and humiliated us enough?"

Sheila turned to me and asked, "What have you to say for yourself, Tina?"

I was too shocked to say anything at first. What had been done in my name was despicable. I knew that I was no angel, but this ugly crime cannot be laid at my feet. I could not even fathom the damage this must have inflicted on my family. My selfishness knew no bounds. I might not have called the police on them, but I was the cause of their humiliation. I could not escape the consequence of my actions.

"Please listen to me. I did not call the police on you. I know I acted like a jerk and said some hateful things to you, but I swear I did not call the police."

Laughing loudly, Sam said, "Do you expect us to believe you? You called the police on our parents when you did not get your way. Why would you not call the police on us when we tried reasoning with you?"

"I swear on my daughters' lives that I never called the police on you. Would you just listen to me? Jalal did not want me to meet you. He and Khadija threatened to do something terrible if I did. I finally convinced them to let me go. I did not know that they would do such a thing to you. Khadija, his wife, was vindictive and a nasty piece of work. She must have planned this. I think they were afraid I will be persuaded by you to leave him. They were afraid that their golden goose will abandon them. I was supporting them with my college money."

"Please, Tina, do not make any excuses. Stop with all your acting. You treated your family, your flesh and blood, like dirt, and you expect us to believe you? What do you take us for? I am sick and tired of you playing the victim. You were nothing but a bully," David said.

"David, I swear I did not call the police on you. I am not blameless either. It was my association with them that had made you targets of Jalal and Khadija. I know what these two were capable of, especially Khadija. She had Jalal wrapped around her little finger. She was a manipulative bitch who made everyone's life miserable. Believe me when I say she was a first-class horror story. She was the one that sucked Jalal into all this. She abused everyone in her life, except her precious son. She beat, berated, and belittled Sahar and Rima. They were shells of little girls before we escaped home."

At this point I could not continue. My memories came rushing back with a vengeance. I had reached my breaking point. I huddled on the floor and started sobbing uncontrollably. I lost sight of where I was and who was watching me. I retreated into another world. A safe place where no one could reach me. I vaguely heard voices asking me if I was all right, but then everything went dark.

Waking Up at the Hospital

I slowly opened my eyes to see that I was in a hospital bed. I turned around and saw my mother dozing on a chair next to my bed.

"Mum," I squeaked.

My mum was jerked awake by my voice. Crying, she said, "Thank God you are awake. You have given us quite a scare."

"How long have I been out of it?"

"A week, my dear. They were worried that you did not want to come back to us."

My mother broke down and started sobbing.

"Mum, Mum, please stop crying."

"Sweetie, we lost you once. We do not want to lose you again. You have kids depending on you. You cannot frighten us like this anymore. You cannot do this to us. We cannot take this anymore."

"Mum."

"Oh, Tina, we love you so much. My heart broke when you left us."

"Mum, I love you too." Taking a deep breath, I asked, "Mum, where are my daughters? Are they okay? Who is taking care of them? They must be terrified without me."

My mum hugged me close.

"They are with your brother, David, and his fiancée, Jill. David felt it would be for the best since the girls know him. Jill agreed with him. The girls are doing well. Sahar and Rima were terrified at first. They thought you left them and did not want them anymore. We had a hard time convincing them that you did not abandon them and will be back soon. Amira is still too young to know what is going

190

on. She is happy as can be bossing all of us around. Jill and David have been great with them."

"Oh Mum." But I could not continue. I was choking from the lump in my throat. Tears started steaming from my eyes. I was bawling like a little kid.

My mum took me in her arms and consoled me.

"Tina, please. Calm down, honey. I know how much you have been through. Both your brothers love you. They were just hurt by your actions. Honey, they have embraced your girls. They understand that you have changed."

"Mum, I swear I never called the police on them. I need you to believe me. I did a lot of horrible things, but I never called the police on them. Khadija must have gotten wind of my meeting them at the café and called the police. She was a nasty piece of work. Mum, you cannot imagine a more vindictive person. She was nasty especially toward Rima and Sahar. She, alongside her son, abused and hurt them. Mum, can you imagine she claimed that these two little girls were sexually enticing their brother? When she wase told he was sexually harassing them?"

"Oh my god, sweetie, what hell have you been in?"

Taking a deep breath to calm myself down, I looked at my mother with sadness in my eyes.

"Mum, you do not know the half of it. It was living hell. I endured much abuse and hurt. Jalal and Khadija treated me like dirt. I was beaten, raped, and blackmailed constantly. I was so broken. I did not want to live anymore. Amira was my only solace. Samira, Jalal's aunt, and her family, were also kind to me. They helped me navigate the many traps Khadija sprung for me. Jalal was a monster. It was only at the end that he realized what a monster he was. The poor girls were such a mess living among these people. I do not know how I survived. I thank God each day that I got out of there in one piece."

My mother started sobbing and could not stop. It broke my heart seeing her this way. She was feeling my pain.

"Mum, please stop crying. I brought all this on myself. I was a selfish, ignorant, ungrateful person. I did not realize how good I had it until I lost everything. You all protected and loved me all my life, but what did I do? I turned my back on you and treated you like the enemy. Mum, I love you all so much. You did not reject me even after all I have done. It is going to take a long time, but I will heal. I need to be strong for myself and my girls. I will not let what happened destroy me. If I collapse, I would have let Khadija and Jalal win. I am stronger than that. I will not fall."

My mother hugged me tight.

"I am so proud of you, my dear. I cannot imagine what you have been through. Rest now, you need to get better soon so that the girls can come later and visit you. They have been asking about you constantly."

I smiled, closed my eyes, and went to sleep.

Waking Up the Second Time

I opened my eyes and saw the most amazing sight in front of me. Both my brothers and significant others were in the room with me. They were all sitting on chairs next to my bed. When I saw their beautiful faces, I started to sob. It was the most beautiful sight in the world. My beloved family here with me.

"Please stop crying, Tina," David said.

I was overwhelmed emotionally. My family here with me at last. I could not stop crying. I was emotionally spent.

"Sis, please stopped crying, we know the truth. Mum could not keep silent anymore and told us all that you have been through. I could not even imagine how you survived such abuse," Sam cried.

I could not stop myself. I was happy my brothers and their significant others were here with me. I was also sad that I have hurt these people so much in the past. I was ashamed to look at Janet and Jill. I knew Jill growing up, but it was the first time I have met Janet. I nearly ruined Janet's mother's life.

"Tina, we need to learn from the past and move on. We cannot live in the past. We need to look to the future. You did a lot of hurtful things in the past, but we need to put them behind us," Janet said.

Taking a deep breath, Janet continued: "You have done many hurtful things to us, I do not want to even pretend that everything is going to be hunky-dory, but we need to try. I know we are not going to be best of friends, but we can try."

I could not believe that I was given this chance to redeem myself in their eyes. This was something I have been praying for. They were willing to meet me halfway. I was not naive enough to think that things would be great between us, but at least they will not shun me. I could not contain my tears. Tears of joy.

"Listen, Tina," Jill said, "I know you and I were never friends, but we can start anew. I will not pretend with you and tell you I will forget all that you have done to me and David, but I am more than willing to try. We want you to come to our wedding. It is a start. We want you to be part of the most important day in our lives. We would like the girls to be our flower girls. We have become attached to them, and I am sure they would love to be part of the bridal party."

"You do not know how much means to me. I never in my whole life expected this. Samar and Sahar were badly abused by their mother and older brother. They always felt unwanted and unloved. Their older brother even tried to sexually abuse them. Their mother, Khadija, claimed that it was their fault." I choked up explaining this to my brothers.

"It is not the right time to get into details, Tina," David chimed in. "We need to focus on your health. We all need to heal from the past. We were all hurt and bruised. We need to take things slowly, and eventually things will work out. Remember, the girls are safe. No one is going to harm them anymore. We would protect them."

"It is time for us to leave, but before we go, someone wants to see you," Jill said.

Sam went to the door and called the nurse over.

"We are going to step out now. Can the girls come and see their mum?"

I heard screeching, and then my little girls barged into the room with Grandma trailing behind them and with Amira in her arms.

"Mama, we were worried about you. Are you okay?" Sahar asked.

"Mama, we missed you so much. Do not leave us again. We promise to be good. Please do not leave us," Rima said and started crying.

Amira, not wanting to be left out, squirmed in my mum's arms, wanting to be put down."

"Mama, Mama, love you," she cried.

All three girls ran to my bed and tried to climb on it.

"Slow down, babies, give me a hug, but do not climb on the bed. It cannot hold us all. I am not going to leave you. I love you all so much."

One by one they gave me hugs and kisses. My mother made sure they did not climb all over me.

"Mum, guess what?" Rima said.

"What, sweetie?"

"We are saying at Uncle David and Aunt Jill's house. We are having a great time. They are so nice to us, but we miss you. We want to go home. We miss our home. We love you, Mum. Please get better soon."

"Girls," Mum said, "we need to return home. Your mother needs her rest. We will come back and visit her tomorrow. In a couple of days, we will bring her home."

They all gave me a hug and a kiss and filed out of the room with my mother.

Another Year Has Passed

I had been home for two years now. I had experienced both great joy and sadness. I had been through a lot, but in the end things improved greatly. My relationship with my family had improved tremendously, but it still is a work in progress. My parents have been there with me through all my tough times. My brothers and their wives have tried putting the past behind them. We were all working hard to strengthen our ties. The girls were instrumental in bridging the gap. My whole family adored them. I was happy that they did not differentiate between Amira and Rima and Sahar. They treated all three girls equally.

I still went to see Dr. Patterson every other week. My mental health had been improving much. My nightmares were less frequent. Sheila had become a friend. She helped me navigate many unresolved issues I had. I was able to function without feeling the weight of the world on my shoulder. I finally was able to forgive myself. I was also able to forgive Jalal for the pain he put me through. I wanted my girls to think kindly of their father.

The older girls asked me about their father. I told them that their father was in heaven and that he loved them very much. They were still too young for them to understand what really happened. I did not want their dad's image to be tarnished. I wanted to protect my girls as much as possible. They rarely asked about their mum or their older brother. It seemed that they still remembered the abuse they endured at their hands. They were worried that I would send them back to live with their relatives back in Iraq. I told them not to worry about that, they were my girls now, and no one would take them away from me.

The girls were thriving in school. I was proud of them. They were honor students. They made friends easily. I enrolled them in different activities. They did ballet and Tae Kwon Do. They loved all the activities. They organized dance performances for Grandpa and Grandma. They loved showing off their dance moves to any willing audience.

My whole family were accepting of the girls, even though they were the daughters of the man who hurt them. They claimed that the girls were innocent of the actions of their father. They had adopted the girls into their family. It was more than I had expected of them. I was proud to be part of such a beautiful and loving family. I wanted to make sure my daughters did not grow up to be like me. I was very loving with them but did not put up with any disrespect or entitlement. They knew they would be punished if they crossed the line. I wanted them to appreciate what they had.

Their paternal uncles and aunts got in touch with them from time to time. They were worried about the girls and wanted to make sure they were doing well. Every time they talked to Rima and Sahar, they questioned them on my treatment of them. They wanted to know if I was raising them in the Muslim faith. They were upset when they realized that I had baptized Amira and was raising her in my faith. They were appeased when I told them that a woman from our local mosque comes once a week to give Rima and Sahar religious lessons.

They were aghast when I told them that I would not force any religion down their throats. It was up to them to follow their own path. They were angry with me, but they were unable to do anything about it. I told them if they wanted to keep in contact with my daughters, they needed to respect my decisions. I was not willing to let them dictate my daughters' lives. I was done being a doormat for Jalal's family. I wanted my daughters to grow up to be strong and independent young women. Jalal's family respected my edicts. They wanted to keep in touch with the girls and were not willing to alienate me. They were also aware of the suffering I had endured at Jalal's hands. It was imperative for them to realize that it was my responsibility to take of my daughters.

Rima and Sahar were as dear to me as if I had birthed them. I did not want anyone dictating their life choices. When they were older, they would have the choice to choose the path they wanted to take. I wanted them to understand that life was not a bed of roses. Each action had a consequence. They were going to be responsible for the choices they make in their lives. I also wanted to make sure that I will not pander to their whims. They knew not to push me too far.

Six months ago, we all attended my brother David's wedding. My girls were so happy to be part of their wedding. It was such a magical day for all of us. Jill looked beautiful as she walked down the aisle on her father's arm toward David. David looked handsome in the front of the church, waiting for his loved one. Sam stood next to him as his best man. Mum and Dad sat next to me on the front pew, proudly looking on their children. It was such a beautiful day.

My girls all looked so pretty in their flower-girl dresses. My twin nephews were the ring bearers. They were all adorable. My twin nephews have become inseparable from my girls. They loved them dearly. Rima and Sahar, being older than Amira and the twins, lorded it over them. They mothered them, but at the same time they took care of them, trying to keep them out of trouble. Amira and the twins were always getting into scraps. They were a menace. I loved seeing them all together. My family, my heart, and my very reason for living.

Ron

I was happy at work. I worked extra hours to make sure I was able to support my daughters. The pay was good, and we wanted for nothing. I had met a fellow nurse, Ron, at the hospital that had shown interest in me. He asked me out on a date. I was hesitant at first. My experience with Jalal had put me off men. I did not want to introduce any man into my daughters' lives. Ron was five years my senior. He had been through a bitter divorce and was the father of two little boys. His ex-wife had left him and their sons for another man. She did not want anything to do with them.

He was a hardworking, family-oriented man. His parents helped look after his boys when he was working. He was working on his MBA and was doing more administrative work. He was doing well for himself. He did not give up his pursuit of me. In the end I accepted to go out on a date. We found that we were very compatible, and our relationship blossomed. My whole family got on well with him. Both our kids adored each other. He asked me to marry him a year into our dating.

We got married a month ago, in a quiet civil ceremony and moved into Ron's large house. We have a beautiful, blended family. Three girls, two boys, two dogs, and a cat all living under the same roof. We are happy. Ron treats my girls as his own. His boys have come to look at me as their mother. We have our ups and downs, but we make it work. Life is good. The nightmares are just a faint memory. I have survived and thrived. I live life to the fullest. I appreciate all the God has blessed me with. I just pray that life is good to all my children.

About the Author

Maria was born and raised in Lebanon. She got a bachelor's degree in political science. In the States, she completed three master's degrees in liberal arts, business, and education. She was an educator for several years. She always wanted to write, and with her husband's encouragement and support, she finished her first book. She has always been fascinated by the effect that religious political movements have on the psyche of their followers. She researched it in-depth, and the story *My Name Is Tina* was conceived. Maria currently lives with her husband in Massachusetts. She loves to read, cook, and take long walks, and she has taken stitching as her latest hobby.

CPSIA information can be obtained
at www.ICGtesting.com
Printed in the USA
LVHW020732290322
714676LV00001B/99

9 781639 850471